WEEKEND TEMPTATION

WEEKEND TEMPTATION

STARFIRE LAKE
BOOK ONE

VIVI PARISH

Editing by Rebecca Fairfax

Proofreading by Kristina Polacco

Cover Art by Naomi Lane

ISBN | Ebook: 979-8-9859408-0-0

ISBN | Paperback: 979-8-9859408-1-7

❀ Created with Vellum

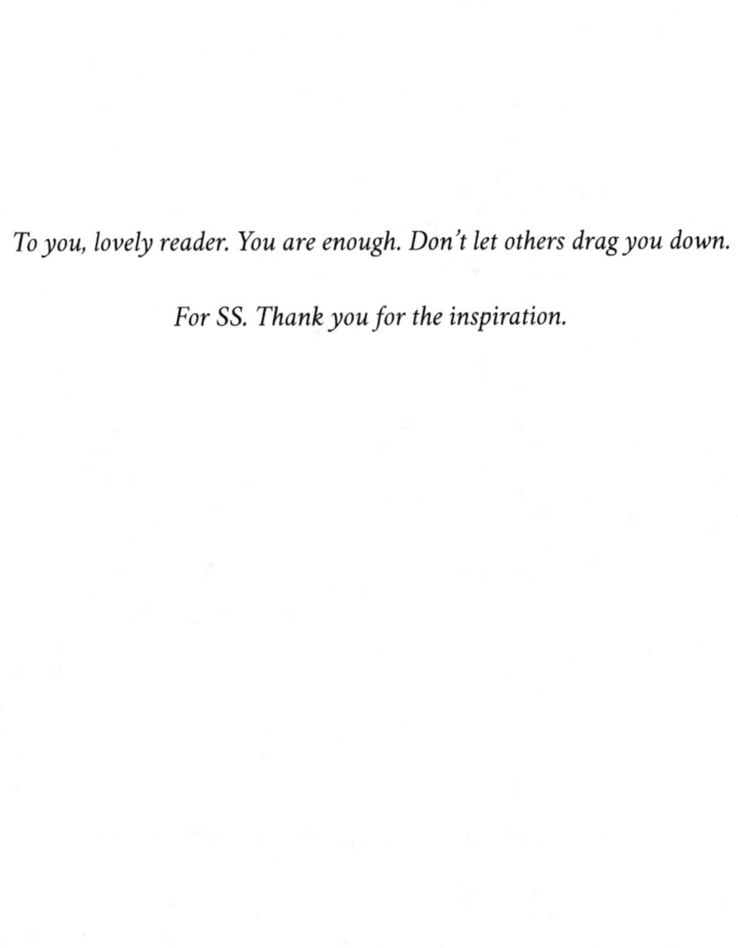

To you, lovely reader. You are enough. Don't let others drag you down.

For SS. Thank you for the inspiration.

CHAPTER 1

Abbie Claret peeked an eye open and caught sight of a bare, muscular shoulder on the other side of the bed. She let her eye flutter closed. She was still dreaming. She had to be. There was no way someone else was in her bed. Abbie hadn't had a man in her bed since her breakup with Jeremy a few weeks ago. Dirty, rotten, cheating ass of an ex-boyfriend Jeremy.

What happened last night? She'd gone out for drinks with some friends she'd made at the Big Apple Fantasy and Comics Convention. Her phone had died after the karaoke bar, and she'd walked to the hotel down the street to get some water and borrow someone's charger. Her plan was to let her phone charge a bit, then walk to the train.

But how had she gotten home? She couldn't pull a memory of the train ride, or even setting up an Uber. Nothing.

Her head throbbed. Abbie pulled the comforter closer. It didn't move. She tugged harder. It still didn't move. *What the hell?*

Irritated, she sat up and *tugged*…and nearly toppled out of bed.

Derek freaking Hartley rolled over, still asleep, and clutched in his hand was a comforter that wasn't hers.

She froze. *Oh. My. God.* She looked around the now-obvious hotel room, and the night before came hurtling back to mind.

He'd been at the hotel bar, and they'd had a few drinks and conversation. And then...

Abbie'd had sex with movie star Derek Hartley.

Hot, fiery, passionate, no-other-man-will-ever-live-up-to-it sex. *Wow. So, not a dream.*

She tried to cover herself with the comforter as much as possible. She couldn't let him find her – what happened last night was clearly a result of drunken insanity. Abbie had no desire to be kicked out of Derek Hartley's hotel room. The walk of shame she was about to do was enough humiliation; no need to add to it.

I need to get out of here. But how? Her clothes were scattered along the floor and furniture, and the very hot movie star was snoring softly less than a foot away. It was adorable that he snored. A tiny flaw in an otherwise seemingly perfect man.

Last night everyone else had loaded into cabs and Ubers, but the train that would take Abbie back home wasn't far; Abbie had told them she was going to have some water and then walk to the train station. She'd done it plenty of times before.

Except last night she didn't go home.

Oh, no. Nope.

She'd found Derek Hartley alone at the bar, large hand wrapped around a glass of amber liquid, and she'd started a conversation.

Abbie had already chatted with him at the convention that week, while she'd run around as a volunteer, helping coordinate lines and panels and such. She'd helped run his autograph table a couple of times, and he'd been funny and easy to work with.

Then last night there he was. A beautiful, lonely man. She'd assumed he was lonely, at least.

A man who isn't lonely wouldn't drink alone at a bar at almost one in the morning.

She'd asked him about his latest project, his favorite place to film, his favorite role. He'd asked her about her job, if she had any pets, did she travel? He'd bought her a couple of drinks. They kept moving in closer and closer during their conversation, until his hand was on her thigh, and hers was on his arm.

Electricity had coursed between them as the conversation turned to the ebb and flow of the loneliness of being single, of the need for human connection, human contact. His knee bumped hers, her hand traced lines on his. Abbie enjoyed being single, making her own choices, and not having to answer to someone all the time. It was mostly okay, until she craved some form of physical connection.

Abbie couldn't remember who had touched who first, or who had kissed who first. But she had another flash...her arm pinned against the wall of the elevator...his lips and teeth grazed across her neck as she watched the numbers crawl higher and higher. A *ding* and his lips were gone, her arm around his waist instead of over her head. Derek leading her down the hotel hallway to his door, his arm around her, mouth against her hair, whispers of sinful things.

She stared at Derek's peaceful face and swore his lips looked swollen. Her fingers touched her own; they were swollen too, and there was some delicious soreness in her muscles.

But Abbie knew better than to stay. Any sort of actual relationship between them would never work. One-night stands with hot movie stars never turn into a happily ever after.

He was Derek freaking Hartley, fan-favorite action star. And she was...Abbie. She had zero desire to become scrutinized by the tabloids and internet. She saw how revered celebrities were, and how quickly that same love could turn into anger and animosity. There was no way she'd measure up. It wasn't what she wanted for her life.

It was better to avoid the awkward goodbye and just disappear. She extracted herself from the comforter and slid off the bed. Abbie crawled on all fours until she found her skirt from last night, tucked under a chair. She rolled onto her back and slid it on. She spotted her bra near the nightstand, on Derek's side of the bed, next to an opened gold foil wrapper. Abbie made her way around the bed and up the other side. She grabbed the bra and hightailed it back to the foot of the bed. She slid on her bra and got it hooked when her shirt dangled in front of her.

"Looking for this?" There was gravel in Derek's voice.

Abbie tilted her head up; blush rushed to her cheeks.

"Uh, yes. Thanks." She went to grab the shirt, but Derek pulled it out of reach.

"Sneaking out?"

Caught red-handed. Just her luck. Not even able to sneak out after the hottest sex of her life. *Figures.*

"No...Just...uh...just getting dressed."

"So that you could sneak out." There was a hint of a grin on Derek's face.

Abbie stayed silent. He wasn't wrong, but she didn't want to admit it.

"You know, it's rude to not even say good morning." The grin got wider.

"I didn't want to wake you." She stood and tried again to grab her shirt, but he again pulled it out of reach.

"A man could get the wrong idea, seeing you sneaking out half dressed. Like maybe he did something wrong."

"Oh, no, no. No."

"So...no?" Derek climbed off the bed and stalked toward her.

She backed up and watched the sheets around his waist slide away. Abbie swallowed hard when she saw the black boxers that did very little to hide his morning erection.

Heat bloomed low in her body, and she backed up even faster, her words tumbling out. "You didn't do anything wrong. You did...a lot of things right. It's just...I should get home, change, get ready for the last day of the convention." Abbie bumped into a chair and went flying.

Strong arms surrounded her and kept her from hitting the floor.

She stared up into ocean-blue eyes and knew if she stayed, she would be ruined forever. There would just be no way for anyone to compete. If she were honest with herself, she was already dancing along the edge of falling for this man. Derek was handsome, funny, and kind. A lot of people underestimated the impact of kindness. The conversation last night flowed easily, and the sex had been earth-shattering.

But that was just a fantasy. It wouldn't work between them, with his life in the spotlight and her desire to not live a life under scrutiny from strangers.

Derek leaned down to whisper, "The last day of the convention was yesterday."

Abbie shivered as his breath caressed her ear. "Right." It had been a small convention, in terms of size; the first one put on by a new company, and it had run from Wednesday to Friday. Which was yesterday.

She backed into a wall, the red and gold wallpaper rubbing against her bare skin. Derek boxed her in with his arms, his hips dangerously close to hers. She felt his chest rise and fall against hers, the thin fabric of her bra doing very little work as a barrier. She ached for him, which was insane. They'd spent some time together during the convention and one night together. Abbie needed to get a grip.

"You could stay."

The impulse and temptation to relive the previous night was almost too good to pass up. *Oh no, stay strong.* "What?"

"Stay. With me, for the weekend."

There was no way he was serious. "What exactly are you proposing?"

A devilish smile crossed Derek's face, and as he trailed a hand up her hip, fire ignited under her skin. "It's a long holiday weekend. If you don't already have plans, I'm thinking four days of no-strings fun. Food, drinks if you want them, and more of what we did last night. A lot more of it...if you're up for it." He raised an eyebrow.

Oh, she was up for the challenge. Even though she knew it was a terrible idea.

Four days of no-strings, no-holds-barred fun, and even more of the best sex of her life with one of the hottest men in the world? There had to be a catch.

"You don't have plans for the holiday weekend?"

Derek shook his head. "My plans fell through earlier this week." He maneuvered his leg between hers, his thigh pressed against her just enough to tease. She almost whimpered. "What do you think? You, me, and a weekend of sin."

Abbie bit her lip. It was tempting, so very tempting. "And after the weekend?"

"Then we go our separate ways."

Abbie was quiet for a few moments. She didn't need to be back at the office until Wednesday, having had the almost prophetic foresight to take off the Tuesday after Memorial Day. There was nobody waiting for her at her one-bedroom apartment, and there was no airline ticket to have to rebook, because the convention had been an hour and a half train ride from home.

This was an insane idea. She was crazy for even considering it.

Derek smiled again, his thigh still between her legs, hand on her hip. He brushed his thumb against the bare skin just above her skirt. She shivered.

Then she remembered the electricity she'd felt every time they'd brushed against each other last night at the bar, and how her heart had fluttered every time he smiled. How his lips had felt against her skin just a few hours ago.

Any shred of self-control she might have had unraveled.

What's the worst that could happen? Chafing?

"I'm in."

CHAPTER 2

A couple of hours later, with newly packed bags in hand, Abbie pressed the elevator button for Derek's floor. *This is so stupid.* She'd texted her best friend, Megan Keating, and told her what she was doing. In typical Megan fashion, her response was *get it, girl.*

Megan had been the one to help Abbie eat too much ice cream and drink too much wine post-Jeremy-break-up. She'd encouraged Abbie to jump at Derek's offer – the perfect weekend to get Abbie out of her funk and just let loose and have fun. Megan was rarely wrong.

The elevator opened, and she headed down the hall to his room. She didn't have a key but knocking felt awkward. *Standing here is even worse.* Two knocks, and a few moments later, the door opened.

"Hi." Derek motioned her in. He wore jeans and a dark red Henley with the sleeves rolled up. Abbie almost swallowed her tongue at the sight of his muscular forearms. While she had gone for casual but sexy with her outfit change, Derek went for casual, but the shirt was just a bit small and hugged his chest.

"Hi." Abbie stepped over the threshold and put her small suit-case down. He closed the door and stepped around her.

Derek leaned in and grinned down at her. "Your lips look a little swollen."

"I can't imagine how they got that way." In a moment of boldness, Abbie reached up on her tiptoes, closing the gap he'd left. She pressed her mouth to his and groaned at the softness. Derek wrapped his arms around her waist and pulled her against him. After a few moments, she stepped away, and he let her.

Derek's hands were still on her hips, though, his grip tight. "I think we're going to have a lot of fun this weekend."

She reached for a hand and went to lead him into the bedroom, eager to have him rip off the shirt and skirt she wore. She saw his bags stacked neatly by the door and turned back to face him. "Are we going somewhere else?"

"Well, the room was only through today, and I requested a late checkout. But I have a house rented." He tilted his head. "Is that okay?"

Alone in a house with Derek Hartley. An image of him fucking her on top of a kitchen table sprang to mind. "Yeah, it's okay." Abbie realized she should maybe be a little afraid of being alone with a strange man. "Uh, just so you know, I have to check in with a friend at least twice a day."

Derek grinned even wider. "Not a problem. Shall we?" He motioned back out to the hall.

He pulled a hat from his bag, put it on and reached for her suitcase.

"Oh, I can get them." The small piece of luggage was mostly filled with the sexiest clothes and undergarments she owned, plus toiletries. The other bag carried her wallet, keys, and ID.

"Nah, I got it. Just close the door behind us?" He grabbed her bag and headed down the hall. She made sure the door clicked shut and followed.

Suddenly nervous, Abbie asked, "Is it okay if we're seen together?"

"I don't think there's anyone around, but if you want to go out ahead of me, that's not a problem. There's a car waiting outside. Driver's name is Paul."

The elevator dinged, and he let her go in first. "Do you want me to meet you in the car?"

She hesitated. Abbie really didn't want to risk her photo being taken with him, not if it meant her face all over social media. The only thing she wanted out of this weekend was amazing sex and multiple orgasms; notoriety was not on her list.

Abbie nodded. Derek winked as the doors shut.

Abbie was thankful for the empty elevator. This was truly insane. Going to a house with Derek Hartley, where it would be just the two of them for the entire long weekend. The sex last night was great - really fucking great if she were honest - but this was still stupid, wasn't it? Leaving the hotel separately and meeting in the car? This weekend was already more complicated than she anticipated.

The *ding* sounded again, and the doors opened. There were paparazzi outside, waiting for Derek. Abbie's knees were weak. The photographers hadn't been there when she arrived, had they? How would they know when he was leaving?

She stepped outside, the brisk spring air enveloping her. The photographers let her through their swarm, and she couldn't help but smile. If they only knew.

A man in a suit stood next to the only car at the curb. A stretch limo. "Paul?"

"Miss." He nodded and opened the car door for her. Abbie glanced back before she slid in. Hopefully the photographers wouldn't realize she was getting in Derek Hartley's private limo. Paul quickly closed the door behind her.

The driver's door opened, and Paul peeked his face through the divider. "Miss? Mr. Hartley suggested we drive around the block and try to make the photogs out there think this is a different car. What do you think?"

"Oh." *Thoughtful.* "If you think it'll work, we can give it a try."

"All right, then." He pulled onto the street and slowly made his way around the block.

"Hey, Paul?"

"Yes, Miss?"

"Will you be the driver all weekend?"

"Just for today, Miss."

"Oh, okay."

"Something I can do for you?"

"No, it's nothing. I was just curious." As Paul drove around the block, Abbie sent a quick text to Megan to let her know the change in plan. Megan had requested the text twice a day to make sure Abbie was safe. *Nothing better than a best friend.*

The limo turned onto the block of the hotel, and Paul expertly double parked in front. "Slide down and duck a little, if you will, Miss." She followed his instruction as he jumped out to open the back door for Derek.

Derek came running out of the hotel, and Paul opened the car door while a hotel employee took their luggage from Derek and put it into the trunk of the limo. Derek waved at some fans across the street and hopped into the back seat. He saw her halfway on the floor in the middle of the limo and laughed.

Once the door was closed and Paul was back in the driver's seat pulling away from the curb, Derek held his hand out to her. She took it and let him lift her up. "Paul, divider up, please."

"Sir."

The tinted glass slid into place, and Derek wrapped his arm around Abbie's waist. "Hi. Sorry about that."

"You don't need to apologize. It's...well, it's your life."

"Sometimes, but not all the time." He nuzzled her neck. "How are you feeling?"

His breath on her neck was distracting. "Hmm?"

"Are you sore from last night?"

Her body ached in ways she hadn't thought possible, but not from soreness. "Not really, no."

"It's a long drive to the house. Or so I'm told." His lips brushed the sensitive spot on her neck. She shivered.

"I wonder what we'll do to pass the time."

Derek slipped his hand up her shirt and skimmed his fingers along her lower back. He licked and nipped the edge of her ear. "Oh, I'm sure we'll think of something. Scrabble, maybe."

"Mm, no. I've never been very good at spelling." Abbie wound her fingers through his hair and dipped her head back, to give him access to her throat. He followed her lead and left a trail of kisses down to her collarbone.

She pulled him up for a kiss and moaned at the feel of his lips against hers. The taste of him was intoxicating. Abbie was tiptoeing a slippery ledge, having sex without strings, but she wanted to let loose just this once. When would an opportunity like this happen again? Limo sex with Derek Hartley?

Derek trailed his fingers up her back and flitted along the edge of her bra. "Trivial Pursuit?"

"Actually, I'm pretty good at trivia."

"Oh yeah?"

"Mhm. For example." Abbie pulled away, and tugged her shirt over her head, revealing the black lace bra. "This opens in the front."

The laugh from Derek was low, and it sent shivers up Abbie's spine. "That's an excellent piece of information to have."

Derek's gaze lingered, and Abbie moved to cover herself.

"Oh, no. Don't do that. You're...perfection." Derek kissed her, long and deep. Need started to build in her again, and she rubbed her hips against him. Derek growled and put one hand on her bra. Without looking, he undid the mechanism, and slid his hand under the fabric to cup her breast. His fingers were gentle but sure in their attention to her already taut nipples.

"Derek..." Abbie was breathless, heat coursing through her veins.

"Yes, Abbie?"

Abbie arched her back, a silent plea. He leaned down, a wicked grin on his face, and took her nipple into his mouth. She clutched his shirt, and her head rolled back onto the seat as his tongue and lips worked magic on her.

"Abbie?"

"Hmm."

"Do you want me to keep going?" He punctuated his question with slow kisses down her bare stomach.

"Yes."

He stopped for a moment and propped his chin on her belly. "Look at me for a second, beautiful."

Abbie let out a breath and lifted herself onto her elbows. "Yes?"

"Will you tell me when to slow down or stop?"

She met his gaze and let herself drown in the blue depths. "Yes, I will tell you when to slow down or stop."

"Do you want me to slow down or stop right now?"

Even if desire wasn't burning through her, she wouldn't want anything except for him to keep going. "No."

Derek smiled, and her heart nearly stopped. He was good-looking on screen and in photos, sure, but this was a different level of beautiful: sharp cheekbones and a strong jaw, and deep blue eyes.

"Good. There are a lot of things I want to do with you. Like tasting and fucking you in the back of this limo." Derek resumed his path of kisses. He skimmed his fingers up her bare leg, from her ankle, along her calf, up the underside of her knee to her thigh.

Abbie couldn't focus on anything except the feeling of Derek. The car rocked, and she grabbed the headrest for support. He found the waistband of her panties, and he slipped them down her legs and onto the floor.

Derek kissed the sensitive spot on her hip, which made Abbie buck just a little. He moved his mouth to her core, gave one stroke of his tongue. "Mm. Sweet as sugar."

Derek licked and sucked, and Abbie lost all sense of reason. She bit her hand to keep herself from moaning too loud.

Her other hand tangled in his hair, and she pleaded with him not to stop. Derek chuckled and kept licking and sucking on the most sensitive part of her. Tension coiled and she was so close. Derek slid a finger into her, then a second, and quickly found the perfect spot to send her climaxing over the edge. Wave after wave of pleasure coursed through her.

A few moments later, she came down from the rush and settled back into herself. Derek rested on her stomach, one of his hands under her ass, the other around her lower back.

"Hi, sweets."

"Hi. That was..."

"Just the beginning."

CHAPTER 3

The house Derek had rented was situated in the small town of Summer Hill, located north of Manhattan, not far from the Connecticut border. It was quaint, if a four-bedroom house with a huge kitchen, pool, and privacy fence could be considered quaint. It was nestled back from the road, a few trees and tall bushes providing even more privacy. But a person walking by would never guess it was rented out regularly to movie stars.

Abbie's favorite room so far, if she had to pick one, was the small library set off the living room. She doubted she'd get to spend too much time in there, but the large chairs looked cozy and inviting, and the floor-to-ceiling bookshelves made the bookworm in her swoon.

"Hey, let's get something to eat. Then we can talk terms."

Abbie spun at the sound of Derek's voice. He leaned against the doorjamb, his arms crossed, sleeves folded up to showcase his forearms. Abbie had a hard time swallowing.

"Terms? I thought we already agreed...this weekend, fun, food, fucking," she punctuated the words by ticking off her fingers. "Then we go our separate ways. Like the Journey song."

He smiled, and Abbie warmed. "That's true, we did. I meant

more along the lines of what we can and can't do in bed, or on the kitchen counter, or on the living room couch, or on any other surface you can think of." He was still in the doorway, but every one of Abbie's nerve endings was on fire. She felt stupid for not realizing earlier. *What did I get myself into?*

"Ah, makes..." She cleared her throat. "Makes sense."

She followed him into the kitchen and sat at the large island. Abbie was no stranger to a kitchen, but her knees were weak, and she didn't trust herself not to slice open a finger.

Derek made them some sandwiches and a small salad, seemingly familiar with the kitchen. Abbie was eager to get the awkward conversation over but had no idea how to start.

"Hope you don't mind turkey. My assistant said this was all they had fresh at the deli, and I don't particularly like ham."

Abbie started at the word 'assistant,' but of course he had one. Derek probably had a full schedule of meetings and travel and rehearsals and who knew what else. It made sense he'd have help. He placed her plate in front of her, and a fork to the side.

She took a bite and nodded. "It's great, thanks." She dug into the sandwich, keenly aware that he watched her. "Sorry, I didn't realize how hungry I was." She ate quickly and finished the sandwich and salad in minutes.

Derek finished eating almost as quickly as she did. "Seems limo sex and multiple orgasms can really work up an appetite."

"I guess so." She took the plate to the sink and rinsed it off.

"Leave it for now. Let's go sit and talk." He gestured to the living room. They settled into the couch, facing each other. Nervous and hyper aware of her short skirt, Abbie tried to find a position that didn't flash too much bare skin.

Derek had one arm along the back of the couch behind her, his fingers playing idly with her hair.

"How about we start with things you don't enjoy?" His voice was soft.

"You've done this before, haven't you?"

"A no-strings-sex weekend with a woman I met only four days ago?" Derek shook his head. "No, this is a first for me."

"Oh." She took a deep breath, her nerves trying to get the better of her. "Well then, maybe not exactly this same situation. But...you've had..." Abbie searched for the right words that wouldn't insult him. "Fun weekends without obligation?"

"A few one-night stands...before my career started to take off and I started getting recognized. College was college, after all. Did you ever have one or two-night stands with anybody?"

Abbie nodded. "Once or twice, until I realized that the guys only wanted to have sex. Then I stopped getting into bed so easily. After that...guys stopped answering texts or phone calls. Or they'd cheat on you after a few months together." *Like Jeremy.*

Another one of the reasons she'd decided to stop dating. It wasn't worth the effort if the guys only wanted sex before they disappeared. She'd ventured into dating apps a couple of times but deleted them after a few days. Sometimes it was better to avoid the difficult navigation between men who wanted to get to know her and men who were only looking for sex.

Except for this weekend. The agenda for the next four days was clear and laid out from the start. Sex with no strings, then a goodbye. It didn't hurt that Derek was hot as hell and made sure she came first. Few others had even made that attempt.

No, this was exactly what Abbie needed.

Derek pushed a loose strand of hair behind her ear, bringing her back to the present moment. "Morons. Their loss is my gain."

Abbie wasn't sure if the compliment was genuine, so she side-stepped it. "Maybe. Or maybe they were just there to pass the time until I figured out what I wanted from a guy, from a relationship."

She'd blamed herself for her ex's infidelity, until Megan threatened to smack her with a spoon. The problem was that Abbie didn't know exactly what she wanted. Abbie knew what she didn't want, but that wasn't the same thing, was it?

"Have you figured it out?"

She shook her head. "Not really. I don't think I'm ready to commit to anyone besides myself right now." She laughed. "Which makes this the perfect weekend."

"It does, does it?" Derek traced down her neck with his fingers, along her collarbone, and down her arm.

"It does. And speaking of...I do have one thing I don't particularly enjoy." Abbie adjusted the hem of her skirt, nerves flittering through her.

"Lay it on me, and we'll avoid it unless you give me the go-ahead."

"I...uh...I don't like anal." Her cheeks flamed, but she pressed on. "I've had boyfriends try it and it just...I don't like it." She waited for Derek's complaint or for him to say that the whole weekend was off.

A small smile crossed Derek's face. "I understand. I doubt they were doing it correctly, but I promise I won't pressure you into it. If you change your mind and want to give it a go, I'd be more than happy to show you how enjoyable it can be."

Relief flooded her. "Thank you. That means a lot. Um, is there anything you don't like?"

He was thoughtful for a moment, fingers still twirling her hair. "I'm a very private person, so no photos or videos this weekend. And no PDA if we do venture out in public."

That was fair, and she'd figured as much. "Agreed. Nobody needs to know about this weekend except us. And my friend Megan." Derek looked like he was about to argue, but she stopped him. "That's just for safety purposes; she isn't going to get any details."

"You sure you don't want to share this with the world?" There was a hint of worry in his eyes. Fear, maybe.

"Positive. I don't like sharing my private life, even when it's not sex with a hot movie star. I sure as hell don't want the tabloids discussing what's going on in my bedroom."

"I'm sorry...'hot movie star?'"

Abbie gave him a playful shove. Derek wrapped his hand around hers, and gently pulled her onto his lap. She felt his arousal pressed against her. Desire flooded her and she rolled her hips, trying for any kind of friction.

"Someone's impatient."

His words were a breath against Abbie's neck. She felt his fingers move along her back, down to the hem of her shirt. She leaned back as Derek lifted it over her head, revealing her bra and bare belly.

"You never did give me back my underwear from the limo, you know. I had to get a fresh pair."

"I do know. It's upstairs in the bedroom."

"Happy to know it's somewhere safe."

He just grinned at her. Abbie's heart fluttered, and she had to remind herself that she could not fall for this man. No matter how easy he might make it.

"So then...there isn't much you don't like?" Her words came out huskier than she intended. But the idea that this gorgeous man was all hers for a long weekend, just there for company and pleasure, was overwhelming.

Derek's lips were on her neck, and he let out a small laugh. "No, there isn't much I don't like. Mostly I just like to make my partner feel good."

He flicked his tongue against her earlobe, and she trembled. Abbie felt his smile against her skin.

"And what about a partner who wants to make you feel good?" Abbie ran her nails along his scalp and down his neck and across his shoulders.

Derek shuddered and growled. "Would you like to see the bedroom again, sweets?"

"Very much, yes."

He kissed her and gave her ass a gentle smack. "Stand up, please."

She did as he asked and squealed as he scooped her up over his shoulder. Derek carried her down the hall and into the bedroom.

She couldn't help the giggle that escaped. "Hmm, the carpet in here is lovely."

Derek laughed and put her down in front of the bed. "You're lovely."

The compliment warmed her, but she tried not to take it to heart. The weekend was about sex, not falling for him.

He kissed her; one hand cupped her chin, the other wrapped around the small of her back. Derek pulled her against him, and she yielded to him, to his lips and tongue. It was a searing kiss, as if he'd been drowning and she was his air.

He pulled away, and she wobbled at the loss of contact. Derek grabbed the back collar of his shirt and tugged it over his head in one smooth motion. Abbie's jaw almost hit the floor. No man she'd been with had ever taken clothes off like that before, but it was her new favorite thing.

"You're…" She motioned to his chest and abs.

Derek looked down at himself then back up at her, his hands out in a questioning gesture.

"Wow."

There was a slight blush on his cheeks as he pulled her against him. But the low rumble that came out of his throat was pure sin. "Get on the bed and spread your legs for me."

Abbie did as he said, removing her skirt in the process, and when she had gotten into place, his pants and boxers were gone. The length of his hard cock was impressive, and Abbie ached for him to fill her.

Derek licked his lips and pulled her to the edge of the bed.

Surprise lit through her. "Oh, again? But you…in the limo…"

Derek leaned over her, his arms on either side of her head. He dipped his head down for a quick kiss. "As if I could ever get enough of the way you taste."

Shock at his declaration and what it could mean was quickly replaced by pleasure as Derek kissed his way down her body and licked and sucked at her core. She lay back on the bed and tangled her fingers in his hair, and gently dragged her nails along his scalp. Derek moaned. She looked down at him, the sight of him between her legs intoxicating.

A delicious tension built tighter and tighter, low in her belly. Abbie moved her hips in time with his strokes. "Don't stop. Please don't stop."

Derek continued his feast, licking and sucking her until starbursts exploded under her skin. Abbie bowed off the bed, pleasure coursing through her, and she shuddered as Derek wrung every bit of the orgasm out of her.

She panted as her climax eased, hungrier for him than ever. Abbie pulled him up to her mouth for a kiss, and whispered against his lips, "I need you inside me, right now."

He disappeared long enough to find a condom and slip it on. Derek was on top of her in moments and slid into her in one slow, smooth motion. Abbie gasped at the fullness and wrapped her legs around his waist, her arms around his neck.

Lost to the feeling of him, Abbie moved her hips and matched him stroke for stroke. She nibbled his ear and licked his neck, delighting in the gasp it elicited from him. She raked her nails along his scalp again, and Derek moaned.

"You feel so good. Fuck."

Abbie arched her back. "Deeper," she whispered against his skin.

Derek obeyed her command. He slid one hand under her and lifted her hips and drove deep. She cried out as another orgasm took her by surprise. A few moments later, Derek followed her over the edge.

They collapsed together on the bed, Derek supported by his arm. He kissed her again before he went to clean up. Abbie took a few minutes before she followed suit, her legs a bit shaky.

Abbie crawled back into bed, having put on the Henley Derek had discarded on the floor earlier, and a fresh pair of underwear. Her body was sated and a little sore. "Do you think we should eat something?"

Derek had already delivered on his promises of multiple orgasms, and it was only the first night of their weekend together.

"Technically, I've already eaten."

She gave him a gentle shove but laughed anyway.

"You know, I hear there are some good restaurants in town. We could have something delivered."

Abbie looked him up and down as he lay on the bed. Derek wore nothing but boxer shorts, one arm above his head and the other resting on her thigh. His fingers played a melody on her skin. Tingles rippled out from where he touched.

"Only if you promise to answer the door wearing exactly what you're wearing right now." She giggled, and he raised an eyebrow at her.

"That's one way to get the town to talk. Though, I do think you'd make a delivery person's entire month if you answered the door wearing that shirt and your underwear and nothing else." Derek rolled over on top of her, pinning her with his hips. He sat up, his weight on his knees, and grinned. "Some improvements could be made."

"Oh?" She was breathless as he reached down and undid the top two buttons on her borrowed shirt.

"Mm." He admired his work and pulled the fabric down her chest a little more, revealing the edge of her areola. "Oh yeah, that'll make their entire year."

"You don't think it's a little much?"

Derek shook his head. "Nope. In fact, it's just enough that I think I'll keep you to myself. I don't always like to share."

Her heart stuttered. A shadow crossed his face, gone as quick as it started. "At least for this weekend." Derek leaned forward and used his teeth to pull the shirt away to reveal the rest of her breast.

Derek wrapped his lips around her already taut nipple, and Abbie sucked in a breath. "Mm." She threaded her fingers through his hair, and as his lips moved down her body, a thought lingered. Yes, this was only for a few days, and she would enjoy every damn moment of it.

She would drink her fill of this beautiful man and hope she didn't die of thirst when it was over.

CHAPTER 4

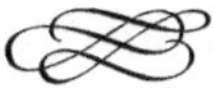

A small snore woke Abbie. The room was dark, and there was a man in bed beside her. *Oh, duh.* Derek. There was an ache in her muscles, and she tried to discreetly stretch it out. Her bladder protested. Abbie rolled out of bed and padded her way to the en suite bathroom.

Once she was done, Abbie tried to slide back in unnoticed. But Derek reached for her. She scooted toward him, and he threw his arm around her waist and pulled her in against his chest. He had stopped snoring, but his breath drifted along her neck. He settled into place, and Abbie waited for his breathing to even out again. It had to be almost dawn, but she couldn't fall back asleep. Instead, she just basked in the darkness and the feel of him against her.

The weekend wasn't supposed to be complicated. Sex, fun, and done. They'd had sex so many times she lost count of the orgasms. Then there was the fact that Derek had made sure she'd eaten, showered, and gotten plenty of rest. And there were still three days left. She was in trouble. If she wasn't careful, she was going to get feelings, and that would just make it complicated.

No, she just needed to focus on the sex and keep emotions

separate. Like a wall between them. Emotions made everything messy and complicated, the exact opposite of the point of this weekend.

Separation of physical and emotional was difficult to imagine with his bare chest against her bare back, and his growing erection behind her.

"Did I wake you, sweets?" His voice was heavy with sleep. It still sent a shiver down her spine.

"No, my bladder did that."

"Mm. What time is it?" He placed a gentle kiss on the nape of her neck. She sighed.

"Too early to be awake. I don't think the sun is even up yet."

"Are you still sleepy?"

"No, I don't think I could fall back asleep." She didn't know how to tell him that the reason she couldn't sleep again was because she was terrified of falling for him. And of her not being pretty enough or smart enough for more than a weekend fling; scared of him breaking her heart.

"You know, I can almost hear your brain going into overdrive."

"I don't know what you mean." She couldn't possibly be that transparent, could she?

"Your body isn't relaxed." Derek pulled against her waist and rolled her onto her back. He propped himself up on his elbow and tilted his head down to look at her. "If you're uncomfortable or unhappy or anything resembling those things, we can call this weekend off. No pressure, and no harm, no foul."

She knew that. If Abbie wanted to go home, Derek would have a car ready for her in less time than it would take to drive home to her small apartment in Starfire Lake. She should probably go.

But Abbie didn't want to. If she was going to be even a sliver of honest with herself, she wanted to see the weekend through, if for no other reason than to have the memory of him and their time together. Even if it would hurt.

If she could keep her fears buried deep, just long enough to get through the next few days, it would be fine. She could fall apart later if she needed to.

Abbie forced herself to meet his gaze. There was barely enough light in the room to make out his eye color, but she knew the shade of blue matched the ocean. "No, no. It's not that. I want to stay, it's just...you're not what I expected."

"I don't know how to respond to that."

"I'm sorry, no. Not in a bad way, not at all. Quite the opposite. I...I've been amazed at this whole day. Really. Future boyfriends have a very high bar to live up to." As soon as she said the words, she wished she could undo them.

Something like jealousy, or possession, darkened Derek's eyes. But it passed quickly. "I don't want to hear about future boyfriends while the only thing separating me from you is the thin layer of your underwear. This weekend you're mine, and I'm yours. Understand?"

Abbie swallowed and nodded. *Focus on this weekend, and nothing beyond that. Three more days.*

"Good. Then let's raise that bar even higher." Derek leaned down, as if to kiss her. He stopped just far enough away that Abbie had to lift her head to complete the kiss, as if to prove that yes, she really wanted this. She wrapped her arms around his neck and went to pull him down on top of her.

Derek lifted her ass and slid his leg between hers. He rested his thigh against the most sensitive part of her, and she couldn't help but rub against him. Abbie bit his lip and threaded her fingers through his hair. She'd always thought he looked better with longer hair. Not necessarily shoulder length, but anything long enough to grab on to.

A moan escaped his lips when she ran her nails along his scalp. He pushed his thigh against her, and Abbie almost whimpered. Her underwear was soaked, and she was throbbing with need.

"You're so fucking wet." Derek took his time kissing his way down her body. She almost bucked off the bed when he licked the sensitive spot on the inside of her thigh. A small laugh came from Derek before he slid a finger up her center.

"Fuck."

She gripped his hair a little tighter, anticipation and desire overtaking any rational thought of being gentle. "Yes. God, yes. Please, yes."

His finger was gone, replaced a moment later by his mouth and tongue. Abbie cried out and lost herself to the sensation. Derek devoured her, worshipped her body as if it were his last meal and he would enjoy every morsel. He drove her to the brink of bliss again and again, building that need higher and higher. Pleasure wound its way through her body, coiling in the center where Derek licked and sucked.

"Please. Derek." She groaned, and grabbed at the sheets, desperate for a lifeline to ground her. Abbie looked down at him. The sight was almost enough to send her over the edge, but he had backed off. "Fuck."

"You have no idea how good you taste." Derek teased a finger at her entrance and slid in and out.

Abbie rode his hand, but he kept pulling back, keeping her on the edge of orgasm. Her body screamed with tension, but all she could do was beg. "Derek, please."

"You're so beautiful when you beg."

"I'm so close."

His mouth was on her, and he slid two fingers inside of her, expertly stroking that sensitive spot. He teased again and again, her body lifting off the bed. He pulled away abruptly.

She fell back onto the bed, trembling with need. "Derek! Fuck."

"Exactly." A feral grin crossed his face, and he reached over to the bedside table. He wasted no time in ripping open the foil packet and putting the condom on. "Roll over, beautiful."

"What?"

"Roll. Over. Ass up." He gave her a gentle smack on the rear, but she still hesitated.

"Uh."

"Don't worry, I'm not going to cross your boundary. But I want to fuck you until you scream my name into the pillows and make you forget the existence of other men. Now, roll over."

Anticipation and need lighting through her, Abbie followed his directions. Embarrassment flooded her at the intake of breath from Derek as he positioned himself behind her. She started to get up, but he put a hand on her back. "Abbie, you're so fucking sexy it'll drive me insane."

Embarrassment turned to courage, into a feeling of power, and she leaned into it. Abbie looked at him over her shoulder and wiggled her ass. "Oh yeah?"

Derek groaned in appreciation. One hand gripping her hips, Derek pulled her against him and wound his other hand into her hair, gently pulling her head back. "Tell me if this hurts, Abbie."

The hint of pain with the promise of pleasure was intoxicating. "It doesn't." She ground her ass against his cock to emphasize her enthusiasm. A whispered 'fuck' escaped him, and he let go of her hair. One hand on her back was instruction to lean down, the other on her hips to keep her ass up.

Abbie wiggled against him again, desperate for friction. For his cock inside her. "I need you to fuck me, Derek."

He lined his cock up at her entrance, the thick head of him teasingly close to entering her. Derek laid himself against her back, one arm braced on the bed while his other hand ghosted around her hip. Her skin burned with need everywhere he touched.

"Please, Derek."

At the sound of his name, he growled and slid himself into

her. A moment later his fingers were at her clit, stroking and playing.

Abbie gripped the sheets beneath her and met him stroke for stroke. "Yes, fuck. Yes." It didn't take long for the tension to coil again, building higher and higher, tighter and tighter, until Derek moved his hips just enough so that his cock struck that perfect spot. The combination of his cock and his fingers playing with her clit drove her over the edge.

Abbie screamed his name into the sheets as the world cracked apart and pleasure consumed her. Derek grabbed her hips and pumped faster against her. A few seconds later his rhythm staggered as he found his own release. They collapsed into each other, breathing heavily. It took Abbie several moments to come back to herself, and she whimpered as Derek pulled himself away to go clean up.

"Sorry, sweets."

"Mm, no reason to say sorry. That was...there don't seem to be words enough to describe it."

Derek kissed her forehead. "I'll have to try harder next time, so you can come up with the right word."

Abbie watched him walk into the bathroom and close the door.

I am in serious trouble.

CHAPTER 5

The space next to Abbie was empty. The comforter had been pulled up and folded over. But there was no man in bed with her.

Abbie grumbled about early mornings and got up and pulled on one of Derek's shirts. The hardwood floor of the hall was cold, but the scent of coffee and bacon kept her from going back for socks.

She turned the corner and had to bite back a gasp. Derek stood in the kitchen in his black boxer-briefs and a navy T-shirt that was at least one size too small. *What is it with actors and too small shirts?*

His back was to her, and he used the spatula in his hand to expertly flip two pancakes from the griddle onto a plate. A pile of bacon sat on another plate, and a bowl of strawberries and blueberries were next to it on the counter.

"Um, good morning."

Derek startled and dropped the third pancake on the floor. "Crap." He looked over at her, a blush across his cheeks. "Uh, hi. I didn't expect you up yet."

"I didn't mean to scare you."

"No, it's okay. I, uh…" He looked down at the floor. "I just feel bad about the pancake. I don't have batter to make more. That was the last one."

Abbie looked at the counter and saw a stack of at least nine pancakes next to the stove. "I think it'll be okay."

"I made coffee, too." Derek motioned to the cabinet next to the refrigerator. "Mugs are in there." He grabbed a roll of paper towels and cleaned up the lost pancake.

Abbie went to help him, but he waved her away. "I've got it. Go sit."

She made herself a cup of coffee with a splash of milk and took a sip. It warmed her from top to bottom, and she sat on one of the tall stools at the island. Derek put an empty plate in front of her with a fork and knife, then brought the rest of the plates and bowls of food.

"You didn't have to do all this, you know."

He shrugged. "I know, but you were still asleep, and I was hungry. I figured you'd also be hungry when you got up."

A piece of bacon landed on her plate, and she took a bite. Crunchy deliciousness filled her senses, and it was as though everything was right in the world. "I take it back. You are now required to do this every morning for the rest of forever." She froze, swallowed, and amended, "For the rest of the weekend."

Abbie almost wanted to take the words back, but the faintest hint of hope refused to let go of that picture. It was a nice image, and what was the harm in imagining it while Derek stood in front of her making breakfast?

A soft smile crossed Derek's face as he waited for her to fill her plate before he grabbed some pancakes and bacon for himself. He topped the pancakes with strawberries, a few blueberries, and a healthy dose of syrup before digging in.

Abbie moaned at the first bite of pancake. "It's delicious. Thank you."

"I'm glad you like it. Pancakes are less universal than some people think."

Abbie shrugged. "I grew up on diner breakfasts, so breakfast food is always a win with me."

"Noted."

She took a few more bites, the sweetness of the strawberries pairing deliciously with the pancakes. The bacon added a nice crunch. "Where did you learn to cook?"

He waved at the food. "This? This is easy. I grew up watching my mom in the kitchen. She was a whiz, and always made enough food in case the neighbors came over. Which they usually did. She taught me everything I know."

"That's nice. My mom could barely boil water." Abbie laughed. "But my uncle owned a diner, so we were always fed. And they never let us pay."

"A diner, huh?"

Abbie nodded. "I love it there. The vinyl seats and the long counter. So much of my schoolwork was done on that counter while Mom was at work." Memories flooded her: the overwhelming smell of bacon as the fry cooks made a bunch in the mornings, the quiet swish of the door between the front end and the kitchen, and the ring and clang of the cash drawer. She smiled softly. "It was also where I had my first date, which in hindsight was a bad idea. But the poor guy didn't know my uncle owned it, just that I loved the food there."

"Sounds like a nice place."

"The best. My cousin took over a few years ago, though my uncle still acts as if he runs the place."

"It can be hard to let go of the things you love, that brought you joy." There was a sadness in his voice. Abbie reached over and brushed his cheek. He leaned into the touch for a moment, then pulled away.

How was she ever going to let him go? They had only spent a

few days together during the convention when she worked with him and helped his handler, and it was now day two of their long weekend together. But oh, Abbie was falling hard and fast. She didn't think she would fit in his world anyway, and a deal was a deal, so she'd enjoy this time with him, then let him go. And hopefully find someone who came even a little close.

"Yeah, it can be. But there's also joy in release and letting go. When the time is right."

Derek took her hand in his and kissed her palm. "What if the time is never right?"

What if the time is never right, indeed? She could only give him a small smile in answer. There was no way Derek felt the same way she did, was there? Unlikely. According to tabloids, his last girl-friend had also been an actress, Katherine Levinson; beautiful and talented. Abbie had seen one or two of her movies and a few interviews. There was no way Abbie could measure up.

Abbie had also seen a ton of negative comments and discussions about Katherine – no topic was off limits to trolls it seemed. That was the last thing Abbie wanted to face.

Derek's smile brought her out of her reverie.

"I have a weird and slightly out of left field question for you, and I'm not sure what you're going to think."

Derek raised an eyebrow. "Very few things will surprise me."

She bit back a smile and asked, "Do we have anything here for baking?" Abbie was met with a moment of stunned silence.

"Baking?"

"Yeah, like cookies. Chocolate chip cookies, to be specific."

"You want to make chocolate chip cookies today?"

"I make chocolate chip cookies every weekend, so I can enjoy them during the week. I bring them into the office and the other paralegals love them."

"Can I ask why you don't buy a package of cookies?"

Abbie shrugged. "Baking calms me. But if I'm trying something new, I'm just worried it'll taste bad. Which only ever happened once, and I was still learning how to convert certain things. Anyway…" She shrugged. "I like to bake cookies on the weekend."

Derek chuckled. "Well, if there's nothing here, I can run into town to pick up what you need." He pointed to a small door next to the kitchen. "I think the pantry is over there."

"I want to come into town with you." Abbie stood and headed to check supplies. "I'm guessing your assistant doesn't get many requests from you for baking supplies?" There wasn't much in the cabinet by way of flour, brown sugar, or baking soda, or even chocolate chips. But she found a small container of salt and some sugar. It was a start.

"Not really, no. You said you want to come with me to the store?" Derek had followed her to the small closet that served as a makeshift pantry. "You find anything here?"

"A few things, but we'll definitely need to go to the store." Abbie looked up at him and caught him staring at her with a look of disbelief. "What?"

"Nothing. Just not what I expected to be doing today."

"Oh." Abbie shuffled on her feet. Anxiety crept over her, and her thoughts came tumbling out. "We don't have to if you'd rather not go into town. It's probably not a good idea anyway, because what if we're seen and people take photos, and it gets posted online –"

Derek gently grabbed her shoulders and turned her to face him. "That's not what I'm saying at all." He cupped her chin and leaned in to brush her lips with his. "In fact, if you bake wearing nothing but an apron and a pair of lacy underwear, I'll even do the dishes."

Abbie's body flushed with heat. "Deal." She wrapped her arms around his neck and kissed him back. Derek's tongue stroked her lips, and she parted them just enough for him to slide it in. He gripped her waist and pulled her closer into his body, his erection pressing against her through his pants.

She took a step back and bit her lip. "Except, I didn't pack an apron, so I'll just have to bake in my underwear." Abbie shrugged and turned to walk back to the bedroom to get ready.

Abbie shivered as Derek growled and followed her.

CHAPTER 6

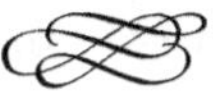

The trip to the small grocery store in town had been uneventful. The store had been surprisingly empty for a Saturday morning on a holiday weekend.

Abbie was grateful for small, weird blessings.

Now she stood in the kitchen wearing nothing but a pair of underwear, as promised, and the bra she'd negotiated since there was no apron to be found. Derek leaned against the counter to her right, arms crossed against his bare chest. During the renegotiation of the baking and underwear agreement, she stipulated that if she was going to be mostly naked, then so was he.

The ingredients and everything they needed were laid out neatly on the island in front of them. There was even an outlet on the side of the island. The perfect kitchen.

She'd found some almost new cookie sheets in one of the cabinets, and after a wash and some wax paper lining, they were ready for cookie dough.

"I'm glad you thought to grab measuring spoons and a hand mixer. But you didn't have to pay for everything."

"I'm more than happy to." He turned to face her, a hand on his hip. Abbie glanced from the corner of her eye. Derek's fingers were dangerously close to the elastic band of his boxer briefs, his cock outlined in the fabric.

She cleared her throat. "Well, I appreciate it."

"Tell me what we're doing here."

"You've never made cookies?"

Derek shook his head. "Not from total scratch like this."

"The correct way to do it is to measure by weight, but...that's not how I do it because I'm not a professional and I don't sell my cookies. So, I just use the regular measuring cups and adjust my measurements a smidge. You're going to love them, I promise."

"I never doubted." Derek licked his lips. Abbie's knees wobbled ever so slightly.

"First thing is to get the flour, salt, and baking soda in a medium bowl together. Measurements are on the bag of chocolate chips. I'll do the butter, sugar, brown sugar, and vanilla."

Derek bumped his hip against hers. "I like it when you're bossy."

"I'll make a note of that for later."

As Derek measured out his ingredients, Abbie got the rest ready for the large bowl serving as a replacement for her stand mixer. They worked together quietly to get everything mixed and laid out on the various cookie sheets, Derek asking the occasional question about why she did something a certain way.

"Because that's how my grandmother taught me," was her most common answer. "Nobody taught you how to bake?" She showed him how to scoop the dough with a spoon and plop it onto the wax-paper-lined baking sheets.

Derek followed suit, with a much larger glob of cookie dough. "I can cook, but my mom didn't do much baking, preferring to order dessert from the bakery. She claimed she was too tired after cooking."

"Grandmother?"

Sadness clouded his face for a moment. "She passed before I

was old enough to learn from her. My mom has a recipe book somewhere, but I never opened it."

They worked together to line their own sheets, and before long they were scraping the bottom of the mixing bowl.

She nodded. "I have a few of those, myself."

Abbie had just placed the sheets in the oven, closed the door, and set the timer on her phone when a small poof of flour exploded on her arm. Derek stood a couple of feet away, a huge grin on his face. He was beautiful, bare chest and toned muscle aside. His smile lit up his eyes, and it took Abbie's breath away. How was she not supposed to fall for this man?

"Oh. Is that how it's going to go? Okay then." She reached for the still open bag of flour and tossed a small handful at Derek's chest. It landed, and Derek let out the most beautiful laugh she'd ever heard, full and free.

He moved so fast she'd barely registered that she needed to run before he snagged the bag of flour and grabbed another handful. She squealed and made a break for the other side of the island, dodging his next toss. Flour bloomed across the front of the refrigerator and swept to the floor.

"No fair, you have the entire bag!"

"Better think ahead next time." He threw another small handful, but she ducked in time. She popped her head up and stuck her tongue out at him.

"I have better uses for your tongue, sweets."

She giggled. "You'll have to put the flour down before that happens."

A wicked grin on his face, Derek put the bag down on the counter behind him, next to the sink, and raised his hands in surrender.

Heart pounding, Abbie stood still as Derek approached. He encircled her waist with his arms, and wiped flour off her cheek. "We've made a bit of a mess, you know."

"Mm. I can't imagine how that happened." She tried and failed to hide a grin as she looked up at him.

"Who knows? But maybe we should clean up a bit." His eyes darkened with desire.

"The cookies are still in the oven." Abbie had to force the words out. It was all she could do not to focus on his fingers on her bare back.

"Mhm." Derek toyed with the lacy edge of her underwear, but he moved his hands up to unclasp her bra and slide it off her shoulders. Abbie let it fall to the floor.

He brushed a thumb along the side of her breast, his eyes never leaving hers. Abbie pulled him down for a kiss.

Their mouths collided and Derek lifted her onto the counter. One hand cupped her breast, the other wrapped around the back of her neck and held her close.

Abbie dragged her nails through his hair, down his back. She reached between them to stroke the hard length of him through his boxers. He moaned and pulled her even closer.

The stove beeped.

Derek groaned. "Are you fucking kidding me right now."

He took a breath, then another, before he stepped away. He grabbed the oven mitts, pulled out the two trays, and set them down on the counter.

Abbie hopped down from the counter. "The cookies might taste better in bed, you know."

Derek licked his lips. "You read my mind." He didn't hesitate as he bent down and picked her up over his shoulder and carried her to the bedroom, cookies forgotten. Abbie laughed and watched flour trail behind them.

CHAPTER 7

"I hope you know that I'm enjoying your company immensely." Derek sat behind Abbie in the extra-large standalone tub. She was nestled between his legs, her back against his chest. He stroked lazy lines up and down her arms.

"Mm, I hadn't realized." Abbie played with the bubbles floating on the surface, winding them in circles back and forth. They'd had another round of sex after baking cookies, and Abbie enjoyed the contentment in their little weekend bubble.

Derek snaked an arm around her side and cupped her breast. "Oh?"

She arched her back, just a bit, reaching into his touch. He toyed with her nipple. "Okay, so, maybe I did notice."

He leaned forward and nibbled her neck. She moaned and rolled her head back. Derek chuckled. "I thought so."

He released her nipple and resumed his original position. "What do you want to do for the rest of the day?"

She shrugged. They'd already had sex twice, and Abbie had stopped trying to count the orgasms. She'd never felt so attended to before. It was like each climax he wrung out of her was a personal accomplishment, or equal to an orgasm of his own.

Abbie sat up and stretched, back arched and arms up. The delicious soreness had eased away in the hot bath. "This bath was a lovely idea, but I think we can find something else to occupy our time. Maybe a swim?"

"Ah, so you did see the pool in the back."

She nodded. "It looks inviting."

"It does, indeed. Though seeing you in a bikini is going to make it difficult to focus on swimming."

Abbie smiled and stood up, exposing herself completely. A few bubbles trailed down her bare legs. "Oh, I don't have a swimsuit." She carefully stepped out of the bath and wrapped a towel around herself.

Derek groaned as he followed her. "You're going to be the death of me."

She giggled and backed up a few steps. Then paused. "The fence is high enough that we don't need to worry, right?"

Derek slung a towel low around his waist and ran his hand through his hair. "The fence is twelve feet high, and the nearest neighbors are a half mile away."

"Good." Abbie grinned and dropped the towel before she ran out of the bathroom. She squealed as Derek caught up just when she rounded the corner into the kitchen. He grabbed her around the waist and spun her around to give her a deep kiss.

His erection pressed against her bare skin. Abbie moaned at the feel of his lips on hers, his tongue sweeping across her mouth, and his hands on her bare skin. There was no way she could get enough of him.

"Do you still want to go for that swim?" His question was soft against her lips.

Abbie looked up at him, "The pool will be there later." She smiled. Derek kissed her again, long and slow, and lifted her onto the still flour-covered kitchen counter.

She moaned as he laid her back and kissed his way down her body, hands tangled in his hair already.

"I can't get enough of the way you taste."

Abbie couldn't think as his tongue reached her hips, her inner thighs… then his lips closed around her clit and gave a gentle suck. She almost bucked off the counter. "Fuck."

Derek slid a finger then another into her wetness. His lips and tongue worked in concert with the expert stroking of his fingers, and it was only a few moments before he was coaxing her body to climax. Stars exploded behind her eyes, and Abbie groaned in pleasure.

She looked down at Derek still between her legs and watched as he licked his fingers.

"You taste so good, Abbie."

Abbie pulled herself up and hopped off the counter. Derek started to step back, but she knelt in front of him and grabbed his cock. "My turn to play."

He gripped her hair and then relaxed his hold. "Is that okay?"

Abbie looked up at him and smiled. "Yes, it is."

"If it's too hard, tap my thigh and I'll let go."

She gave him a wicked grin and nodded. Abbie held his gaze as she licked his cock from base to tip in one long, slow stroke.

"Fuuuuuuck." Derek's head fell back as he threaded one hand through her hair again, and he gripped the edge of the counter for support with the other.

She loved the feel of him in her mouth, and the power that came from giving him pleasure. Relished it, as she licked and sucked the long length of him.

"Abbie, I'm not going to last much longer." Derek's voice was breathless, and his knees shook. Abbie didn't let up, eager to give him his release the way he'd given her so many.

"Fuck, yes. Yes. Oh god, fuck." Derek's grip on her hair tightened then went loose as his body shuddered and he came inside her mouth. Abbie made sure to lick and suck and swallow every ounce of his orgasm out of him. When she was sure Derek was fully satisfied, Abbie stood with a grin on her face.

"You are the most amazing woman, Abbie." Derek pulled her in for a kiss. It was soft and sweet, and Abbie wondered again how she was ever going to let him go.

CHAPTER 8

The couch was even more comfortable when snuggled beneath a blanket with a pillow under her head. Derek had lain down on the other side of the L-shape with his own pillow and blanket. She had started on the opposite side, but somehow had ended up with her head in his lap.

Earlier, Derek had shooed her into a shower while he cleaned up the kitchen. He'd taken a quick shower while she made them an easy pasta and chicken dinner. A plate of cookies now sat within arm's reach on the ottoman.

The movie was one of the action films they both liked; they'd spent the last hour breaking down the different aspects of the story and characters, and Derek explained some of the stunts. As they spoke, Derek had played with her hair, and it was lucky she hadn't fallen asleep.

The hero of the film pulled off a particularly outrageous stunt that made Abbie cringe. It looked impossible without some sort of rig to help the execution.

"Did you audition for that role?"

"I did, but they obviously passed. It was the right move."

"I can't imagine that being true." She gave him a light tap on the leg.

"I went on to different projects, ones that I wouldn't have been able to do. I have some fun indie stuff coming out soon."

"That is pretty exciting."

"Plus, the studio wanted a huge multi-year commitment. I wasn't ready to do that."

"Would you do it now?"

"If they offered me the right part, I'd give it more consideration than I did a few years ago."

"What changed?"

"The market, and my interest, if I'm being honest."

Abbie reached for a cookie. "I don't know if I could be an actress."

"Why not?"

"The surface of the industry makes it look all glamorous, but it also seems like a lot of rejection." She blew out a breath. "I don't think I'd ever be good enough anyway."

"You can do anything you want. But it is a tough business, that's for sure. Rejection hurts, even after years of it thickening your skin."

"How do you deal with it?" Abbie hoped it wasn't obvious she was asking for herself, not curiosity.

Derek was quiet for a few heartbeats. "I feel it. I let myself feel the hurt for a day or two. Then I try to let it go. Having a good group of friends, both in and out of the industry, helps a lot. They keep my head straight."

Abbie looked up at him as a pang of jealousy hit her at the mention of his friends. She would only ever get to have this weekend with him. It started to feel like there wasn't enough time. But that was ridiculous, wasn't it? It was only ever going to be a weekend.

"I don't think I could handle all the vitriol that gets tossed around about celebrities. It seems so invasive."

He sighed. "That's my least favorite part about my career. I try to be on social media to help bring attention to causes I care about, but the negativity can be overwhelming."

"I've seen fans turn on their favorite actors or musicians who then step back from social media. It's like – there's no winning. It's horrible." There was no way Abbie could imagine her life constantly under criticism from people all over the country – or even all over the world. She had enough criticism in her life as it was; there was no need to add to it.

"There isn't. It's why I've stepped back a bit and made the decision for *me*. That's all I can do. Everything else is noise."

Abbie let that thought sink in as she studied him. Derek's eyes were on the screen, but he still played with her hair. He seemed completely content in the moment, and Abbie had to admit she enjoyed spending time with him outside the bedroom. She was hit with a yearning to know more about him.

If she only had this weekend, she would make the most of it in every way she could. "Is there a role that you wish you had gotten?"

"I try not to dwell on that; being turned down for something stings for a while."

She bit her lip, another question hanging in her mind. But she wasn't sure if it was too personal.

"Ask, sweets. I don't have to answer, but you can ask."

"How did you know I wanted to ask another one?"

Derek's finger freed her bottom lip from where she'd been biting down. His tongue slid across his mouth, the barest of smiles. She swallowed hard at the sight.

"What's your question?"

"What is your secret dream role?"

He laughed. "That's classified."

"I promise not to tell anyone ever, even if you do get to do it."

"If I see a headline next week that says, 'Derek Hartley secretly wants to play X in a movie,' I'm gonna know it's you."

"Exactly, so there's motivation for me to keep my mouth shut about it."

He took a deep breath. "I'll tell you, if you tell me a secret, too."

"Assured mutual destruction."

Derek nodded. "Exactly."

"It could also be called mutual blackmail," Abbie pointed out.

"Whatever term you prefer."

Abbie thought about it, then nodded. "You have a deal." She held out her hand and they shook on it, his large hand enveloping hers.

"My secret dream role is to be the lead in a romcom. One of those cheesy but classic movies that everyone says are terrible but secretly love."

"Like *The Proposal*?"

"Yeah."

Abbie sat up and stared at him. The chiseled jaw, the blue eyes, even his hair…he was made to be a romantic lead. She couldn't believe he'd never done one. "You would be excellent as a romcom lead. Why have you not already been cast in a dozen of those movies?!"

Derek shrugged. "I audition, but nobody's called."

"Stupid movie execs."

He gave her a nudge. "Okay, your turn. Tell me a secret."

"Do you have any particular probing question in mind for me to answer?"

Derek looked away, then back at her. "I can't think of anything, so you choose what secret you want to tell me."

"Okay, let me think for a second." Abbie wanted to be honest and give him a secret at least close in measure to the one he gave her. She went for a secret she'd never shared with anyone, not even her best friend, Megan.

Abbie looked down and picked at the blanket. "I've never been in love."

"What do you mean?"

She shrugged. "I've had boyfriends and lovers, even one-night stands. I've cared about them, sure, but I was never *in love* with any of them. Not the way the romance books and the movies make it seem. That all-consuming need to have someone in my life – it's never happened."

"Maybe it'll happen soon."

"Maybe." She took another deep breath. Being vulnerable in front of people wasn't something Abbie usually did, but Derek made space for her to do or say whatever she felt. He didn't push, and always respected her boundaries. Abbie realized she was more comfortable with him than with a lot of people in her life. The two glasses of wine she'd had with dinner must have still been influencing her, but she went for complete honesty.

"The real secret is that even though I tell everyone I'm fine being single, and that I like my life – and I do – I'm lonely. I wouldn't mind a partner, someone to lean on, or spend time with, you know?"

She chanced a glance up at him and found him staring into the distance.

"I do know. It's hard to be single, sometimes."

"It is. Even when it's the better-for-right-now choice. I really do believe it's better to be alone than with the wrong person. Sometimes it feels like I'll never measure up or be good enough for someone to fall in love with. But that doesn't mean it doesn't get lonely." Abbie sighed.

Derek snaked an arm around her waist, and she leaned into his touch. "You're not alone right now, Abbie."

His body was warm, and Abbie loved the feeling of his chest rising and falling under her fingers. She pushed her blanket aside, sat up to straddle his waist, and ran her fingers through his hair. He looked up at her, his blue eyes unreadable. "No, I'm certainly not."

As she leaned down to kiss him, he wrapped his arms around

her waist and lifted her, adjusting how she sat so that when she settled back down his hard length was against her core.

Derek kissed and nipped at her neck. She tugged at his shirt, a blue Henley that she loved, and lifted it over his head. Abbie didn't have long to stare at his bare chest before he'd pressed up against her and reached again for that sensitive spot just above her shoulder.

Abbie rolled her hips a few times, and Derek growled. "That's it, Abbie, ride me."

"It'd be easier to do without all these clothes in the way." She was breathless, need driving her movements instead of rational thought.

"That's a problem we can fix." Derek lifted her up, hands on her ass, and she wrapped her legs around his waist. He chuckled, low and rough, and laid her on the couch.

She arched her back and hissed as he lifted her shirt and trailed soft kisses down her belly. He undid the belt and buttons and slid her shorts off her legs. Desire darkened his eyes when he saw the pink lacy underwear she'd chosen after her shower.

"I'm wearing the matching bra; in case you're interested." She trailed her fingers along her collarbone and neckline.

Derek lifted her so she could pull off her shirt. She lay back down, rubbing one of her legs against his body, inviting him in.

"You're exquisite in pink, but this is still too many clothes, don't you think?"

"You're wearing more clothes than I am, Derek." She gave a pointed look at his jeans. He grinned at her and stood to shuck them off. He pulled the gold foil packet from the back pocket and left the clothes on the floor.

She laughed. "You're prepared, carrying that around." Abbie sat up and plucked the packet from his fingers.

"I do like to be prepared." Derek climbed back on the couch and settled himself on his knees in front of her.

Abbie looked up at him, the packet in one hand, and grasped

him with her other hand. She stroked the length of him, once, twice, and watched as the muscle in his jaw clenched. She teased her fingers up the underside and circled around his tip.

Derek hissed in a breath, eyes on her, mouth open. "Fuck."

A rush of power and desire went through her. "Not quite yet." Abbie positioned herself on her knees and took him into her mouth. She stroked with her hand as she sucked him deeper and deeper.

Derek's hands were in her hair, his breathing heavy. He pulled her up for a kiss, his tongue against hers, one hand splayed across her lower back.

Abbie broke away long enough to open the packet and slide the condom down his cock. Derek watched, and Abbie did not break eye contact.

"That's perfect, sweets." He bent down to capture her mouth.

Abbie stopped him and nipped at his mouth. "Why do you call me sweets?"

Derek licked his lips and stroked her cheek with one hand. He trailed his other hand down to her slit and slid a finger inside. "Because"—he lifted that same finger to his mouth and sucked it — "you taste sweeter than sin."

A thrill of desire sparked through her. Derek leaned forward, and Abbie followed the silent instruction to lie back. He hooked one arm under her leg and pressed himself against her opening.

Derek kissed her again, his tongue dancing with hers. Abbie moved her hips, trying desperately to get him inside her. "Please, Derek."

Derek held her gaze as he slid himself into her. Abbie gasped at the fullness, still not quite used to the size of him.

He kissed her again as he moved his hips. The rhythm was slow but careful. Abbie reveled in the feeling of him on top of her, his strong body moving in time to their heartbeats, their lips pressing against whatever skin they could find.

He lowered himself and buried his head in her neck, nibbling and kissing the sensitive spot under her ear.

Abbie wrapped her arms around him and held on tight. She nibbled his ear, her breathing rapid as her hips met his stroke for stroke. The orgasm started to build, and build, and build. Derek kept his pace steady and drove her to the edge again and again, until she begged him. "Harder, deeper, please. Derek, I'm so close. Fuck me hard."

His hips went from sweet and steady to hard and deep. Abbie moaned and moved a hand to play with her clit. It didn't take long to get to the precipice again, and Abbie shuddered and splintered apart. A few seconds later, Derek groaned against her neck and followed her over the edge.

Derek pulled her onto his chest, and Abbie had never reached such a level of contentment.

She delighted in his little intakes of breath as she trailed her fingers in a lazy map along his chest and abdomen. She loved the tickle of the hair on his chest followed by the smooth planes of his muscles and the dip between his hips.

Abbie wanted to get out the sketchbook she'd tucked into her bag, to commit the beauty and strength of him to paper.

Derek's voice was soft in her ear. "This weekend is going by too quickly. How am I going to give you up?"

Abbie touched her forehead to his. "I don't know. I don't want the weekend to end, either."

She had no idea how they were supposed to walk away from each other after this weekend. It wasn't supposed to be this emotional. Abbie didn't know how to trust again after the heart-break and betrayal of her last boyfriend. This weekend fling was supposed to be just a fling. What did she have to offer someone like Derek, who had a successful career and jet-setting life, beyond a weekend of no-strings fun?

CHAPTER 9

Abbie couldn't get enough of the kitchen in this house. The L-shaped counter against the wall was large enough to keep most of the daily-use appliances out, and the island was spacious enough to do prep work, roll out dough, or even lie back on while Derek took his time feasting on her.

They hadn't spoken again about their feelings after their admissions on the couch last night, and Abbie wasn't going to be the first one to bring it up. Not yet anyway.

It was their last full day together, and there had been an unspoken agreement between them to make the most out of it. She'd go home tomorrow.

Derek had taken it to mean: give Abbie as many orgasms in a day as was humanly possible. She was not one to complain.

"Derek, I don't know if I have another one in me." She was sweaty, breathless, and boneless.

He paused and looked up at her. "Do you want me to stop?"

She propped herself up on her elbows and took in the sight of him: hair disheveled, sweat gleaming on his bare chest. "No, I don't want you to stop."

He growled. Shivers skittered along her spine. Without

breaking eye contact, he licked her center. His tongue flicked her clit again, and again. He slid two fingers into her and started to stroke her most sensitive spot. The orgasm built, low in her belly.

She threw her head back and her body trembled.

"That's it, Abbie, nice and slow."

The pressure built and built, coiling tighter and tighter. Abbie's leg shook. "Oh, fuck."

Derek kept the same pace, drawing out her orgasm.

"Please, Derek."

One stroke, two, his mouth on her clit, and her body splintered into a thousand shining pieces. Wave after wave crested, and Derek didn't let up until she begged him to.

She gave him a sleepy smile. "That was incredible."

Derek leaned over her and kissed her on the forehead. He helped her sit up and handed her the underwear he'd pulled off with his teeth earlier.

Abbie eased herself off the counter, did a quick cleanup, slipped on her underwear, and sat in one of the stools.

Derek moved the towel she'd been lying on and tossed it in front of the door that led to the laundry room. "So, what would you like for breakfast?"

"Breakfast? Isn't it, like, lunch time already?"

"Even though I hate the word, let's call it brunch and have French toast."

Abbie smiled. "Excellent idea. If you give me a few minutes, I can help cook."

"I wouldn't dream of it. Keep your lovely ass right there and relax."

Derek moved around the kitchen to get everything together for their meal, and Abbie took the opportunity to use the bathroom before she grabbed her sketchbook and pencils from the bedroom.

"Do you mind if I sketch while you cook?"

Derek shook his head. "Not at all."

Abbie opened to a fresh page and put pencil to paper. She sketched Derek's eyes, his mouth, his hands. The lines came easy to her, and Abbie barely had to look up at Derek for reference.

At some point, Derek had come over and watched her work. "You're talented, Abbie."

She blushed. "Thanks. These are just warm-ups, not really all that impressive."

"Don't put yourself down. I can barely draw a stick figure. You have talent and skill."

She closed the sketchbook and gave him a smile. "Well, thank you."

Derek's gaze lingered on her for a few extra moments, as if he wanted to say something else. Her stomach growled and he looked away. "Food's ready."

"You know, a girl could get used to morning sex and a hot man making French toast for her."

Derek laughed. "Yeah? Well then, it's a shame the weekend isn't longer."

Abbie couldn't decide whether she was relieved or sad at his joking comment. It wasn't as though he was suggesting they continue seeing each other either. That was enough of an answer to her unasked question about a possible future together. Abbie'd had enough rejection in her life that she didn't want to experience it from Derek, too.

His life was the antithesis of what she wanted – at least the very public part of his life was. The sex, the baking, the humor, his smile, his warmth – those were all things she'd been looking for in a partner. Someone who made her feel safe and like she didn't have to prove that she was worthy of attention and love. Not one of her exes had made her feel anything close to how Derek made her feel.

Derek broke the extended silence first. "Life is weird. Thank goodness for French toast."

"Indeed. French toast and bacon."

He bopped his forehead. "Ah, we don't have any *bacon!*"

"No, no. We don't need it; I was just adding to your declaration. You can't make a sweeping statement about breakfast food and not include bacon."

"French toast and bacon are the superior foods."

Abbie hesitated, unsure of how much of her heart she wanted on her sleeve. "You would love the food at my cousin's diner."

"Good breakfast food?"

"Voted best on Long Island three years running. They changed the menu around when my cousin took over. He added some new things that the customers went crazy over."

"Oh yeah? I'll have to try it some time."

If they were in a real relationship, they could go together. On a date. Eventually.

Derek nudged her with his shoulder. "You okay, Abbie?"

"Yeah." Derek looked skeptical, so she tried to change the subject. "Thinking about how much I wish we had bacon."

Derek laughed and reached for her hand. He gazed at her, an unreadable expression on his face.

"I've had a great time with you this weekend, Abbie. I didn't know what to expect, but I didn't think it would be this hard today."

Abbie didn't know what to say. The weekend had exceeded any expectation she'd set for it, which had been a simple 'have a lot of sex.' "You've surprised me in a lot of ways, Derek. I'm having a hard time, too."

There were celebrities that were able to keep their private lives private, right? Whose partners and spouses weren't in the same spotlight? Maybe she and Derek could find a way. Abbie wasn't ready to put herself out there yet, but hope sprouted as a little bud in her heart.

CHAPTER 10

The water was a little on the cool side, but Abbie dipped into the pool anyway. She hadn't been swimming in ages and forgot how much she loved to float and just stare up at the sky. The clouds rolled by, lazy on their journey to the horizon.

Derek had gone inside for refreshments and snacks. Abbie listened to the wind in the trees, the birds chirping to one other. It was so quiet, and she loved it. It was an acute difference from the area around her apartment, where it was a regular musical of honks, yells, sirens from the too close fire house, and loud exhausts on muscle cars.

"Drinks and snacks are on the table, sweets."

"Thanks!"

"Do you want me to bring anything to you?"

"Actually, a bottle of water and some pretzels would be amazing right now." She maneuvered herself over to the edge and laid her arms on the rough concrete. He brought the bottle of water and a small bowl with pretzels and placed them in front of her. "Thanks, this is great."

"A man could get used to watching you swim naked, Abbie."

"Normally I swim in a bikini."

"A little stringy one?"

She laughed. "Just a regular one, actually."

"I bet you have every man on the beach lusting after you when you wear it."

"Not usually, no."

"You seem to be oblivious to the effect you have on men, Abbie."

Abbie indicated his cock, which was already starting to harden again. "You're giving me a front-row-seat education."

Derek just shook his head and laughed to himself. Abbie watched as he stood and walked to the other end of the pool, then dove in off the small diving board. Abbie bit her lip as he glided through the water and came up for air a few feet away. He swam up to her and caged her in with his arms.

"You didn't notice the cashier at the store checking you out the other day?"

"I have no idea what you're talking about."

"Dude didn't even notice me because he was so busy staring at you." He leaned in and placed a wet kiss on her neck.

"Maybe he was staring at one of my many new hickeys."

Derek laughed against her neck. "He can't see where I'm leaving hickeys, sweets." His voice was gravelly, and it sent shivers down her spine.

She laughed and pushed him away. He let himself float back, and just watched her. He bit his lip and smiled.

The intensity of his gaze made her self-conscious. "What?"

"Just soaking in the last of the weekend." There was a hint of sadness in his voice that Abbie didn't know how to process. Should she tell him that she didn't want the weekend to end? How much she wanted to try for something real? Self-doubt plagued her. What if he was just saying the right things, and didn't mean any of them?

She turned to grab another couple of pretzels. The bowl was

almost empty. "Hmm. Can we order dinner soon? We should have gotten more stuff at the store."

"I was too distracted by your ass in the shorts you were wearing to think of eating anything other than you."

She blushed from head to toe. "Oh."

"But if you're hungry, we can get something delivered from town." Derek floated close again, his strong arms keeping a steady rhythm in the water.

Abbie wrapped her legs around his hips, his cock against her throbbing pussy. "I like a man who takes charge."

"You keep talking like that and I might forget about food entirely." Derek spun them around in the water, so his back faced the edge of the pool, and he lifted Abbie's hips so the tip of his cock was pressed against her entrance. "Though sex *in* the pool is not the greatest idea."

She gave him a wicked grin and lay so she half floated on her back and half rode his waist. Abbie knew the view of her body would drive him crazy. He cursed under his breath.

"If we weren't in this pool right now, Abbie, I'd already be inside you."

She lifted her head to look at him. "Promises, promises."

"Tell me something; do you want me to fuck you, or do you want to go and order food?"

"I do believe I was promised a weekend of fucking *and* food." She wiggled her hips a little. Derek groaned and pulled her in close for a deep kiss. His tongue caressed her lips and she sighed. The weightlessness of the water combined with his strong arms around her was a strange mix, but Abbie only wanted more of him.

"I hate to admit this, but I'm going to need food first." His stomach growled, and Abbie's followed suit.

"Food first it is."

A little under an hour later, Abbie and Derek sat at the table on the veranda, pizza box open and plates full.

Derek closed his eyes as he bit into his second slice. "This is the best pizza place around. I'm ordering from them for the rest of the time I'm in town."

Abbie stilled. He wasn't leaving tomorrow like she was? He was still going to be here by himself? Well, maybe not *alone* alone, with assistants and whatnot, but still.

She recalled something from their chat at the bar before he'd brought her up to his hotel room. "Wait, I thought you had to go to London soon?"

"I do, but I rented the house out until Thursday. I'm gearing up to do another three-month shoot. Next week I have a few preliminary meetings and filming starts at the end of next month. Production and filming get insane, and I wanted to get some prep and time alone in before I went over. It's taken me a long time to get to that point where I know to schedule it in."

Abbie was stunned. Not that he didn't ask her to stay; their long weekend was supposed to be just the weekend, after all. But that he purposefully took time for himself before diving into a project. "That's incredibly self-aware."

"You sound surprised."

Abbie cringed to admit it. "I kind of am?" She rushed to continue. "Nothing against you personally, I swear. It's just that I'm not always even aware of when I need alone time, before my body forces me to take it, you know? I've been working on that. It's hard as hell. It was more of a kudos statement, than anything."

"It's a relatively new thing I'm doing, so, thank you for the kudos."

"Oh? How new?"

"This is only the second time I've scheduled it ahead of production, actually built it into my schedule."

"Gotta start somewhere."

"I saw the short break between the convention and production starting, so I took advantage of it. They would have wanted me there yesterday if they'd had their way." Only two days after an intense three-day experience at a convention doing autographs, photo ops, and meet and greets.

"That's not a lot of downtime."

"No, it's not. Which is why I told my manager I really needed this break." He nudged her again. "I'm so glad I did."

"I am, too. It would have been awkward to have been kicked out of your hotel room instead of you offering a weekend of sex."

"Technically, you were trying to sneak out, if I remember correctly." He brushed a strand of hair away from her face. "I couldn't let you leave without knowing I'd see you again somehow."

Her pulse pounded in her ears. "And now?" Her mouth went dry as she waited for him to say something. Anything, even if it broke her heart.

"I still don't know what I'm going to do." He leaned in and kissed her. His lips were soft, inviting.

She decided to take the leap and follow her heart. The worst he could say was no, and even if it shattered her, Abbie would rather move on knowing she'd tried. "You could pay a visit the next time you're in town."

Derek kissed her jaw. Her neck. "For breakfast?" His breath was a whisper on her skin, sending goosebumps down her arms.

"For breakfast. Or anything else you might want to eat."

He growled in her ear. "Is that invitation good for this moment?"

She nodded. "Consider it open-ended."

"Good. I'm starved." He picked her up, one arm supporting her back, the other under her knees, and carried her into the house down the hall to the bedroom.

Abbie wrapped her arms around his neck and nuzzled the spot under his ear. "The pizza is going to get cold."

"We'll order more."

CHAPTER 11

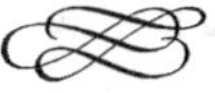

Abbie woke up on the last morning of the long weekend and just lay in bed. The sheets were around her waist, and she was still on her belly. She tucked an arm up under the pillow and studied Derek.

He slept on his side, facing her, his face relaxed. He'd earned his rest, after making doubly sure she was more than sated until the wee hours.

He was beautiful, and she was going home today. Overcome with the urge to create something more tangible as a memory, Abbie slid out of bed, careful not to make noise or wake him. She grabbed her sketchbook and pencils and crawled back into bed.

On paper, she traced the outline of his body: one arm tucked under his head, the other resting on the bed, his torso and abdomen, the contours of his waist and hips, the covers rumpled during sleep, hiding his cock. She took her time lining his eyes and full lips, the curve of his nose and the sharp line of his jaw.

There was a melancholy settling on her, and she did not want to examine why. As she sketched, every thought she hadn't wanted to face came rushing through.

This was only ever going to be a fun weekend, nothing more.

There wasn't a way for them to make a relationship work, anyway. And no matter how many orgasms he gave her, Derek had been clear from the start that this arrangement had a time limit.

Abbie doubted he would want to be tied down, not when it seemed like he had so many commitments to his career. She sighed and continued to work on her sketch, adding shading and depth. How on earth was she going to say goodbye to Derek? She could order a ride and sneak out before he woke up.

Coward.

Definitely. But facing him and saying goodbye, knowing she'd never get to kiss him again...it was harder than she'd thought it would be.

But that was what she'd wanted, too, wasn't it? Just a fun weekend with a hot guy and guaranteed orgasms? It had seemed the perfect setup.

Abbie didn't know why she thought she could have a weekend full of hot sex and just go back to her life. She was such a fool.

Her life was quiet, sure, but she had friends and a job that paid her bills, and her still-new art business. It could be enough. *Hot sex does not a relationship make.*

Then Derek had to come swooning in and mess it all up.

Abbie studied her sketch and compared it to the real thing in front of her. His face was slack from sleep, lips parted slightly, his hair messy. Derek had such soft hair, and she loved that it was just long enough for her to run her fingers through. She resisted the urge, closed the sketchbook, and placed it and the pencils on the floor.

As Abbie turned onto her stomach, she knew her messy emotions were her own fault. She was the one who'd initiated the conversation at the bar. She'd agreed to go up to his room, and she'd agreed to the whole weekend together. Everything came down to her.

Regret was hard to find, and she didn't think she'd ever regret the weekend. Except maybe when her heart broke into a million pieces. She'd fall apart later. For now, she'd enjoy the rest of his company, for as long as she had it.

Such a fool.

Derek stirred next to her, and she smiled as he opened his eyes.

"Morning, sleepyhead."

"Morning, sweets." Derek rolled on top of her and kissed his way down her back. She almost purred in pleasure. "What time is it?"

"Almost seven, I think."

"Are you sore from last night?" He stopped before the blanket that still covered her ass and kissed his way up again. It was their last few hours together. She wanted to squeeze as much out of every moment as she could.

She shook her head. "I'm surprised you're not exhausted. We were up very late."

Derek murmured something against her shoulder blade. His cock hardened against her ass.

"Can you say that again?" She started to roll over, but Derek put his hand on her hip.

"I said"—he brushed hair away from her neck and nibbled—"I want to feel you come around my cock again." As if in agreement, his cock twitched against her ass.

His words had her pulsing in anticipation. One more time, to say goodbye. Abbie ground against him. "Yes." Her voice was breathless.

Abbie had expected Derek to flip her over and start to ravish her. Instead, he continued his slow ministrations. Abbie reveled in the feel of his fingers on her back, his lips on her skin, and the weight of him against her. Each caress, each lick, increased her need, driving her mad.

"Roll over, beautiful."

Abbie obeyed. She reached for him, but Derek pinned her

hands to the pillow above her head. "No touching." He brushed his nose along her neck. "I want to savor you."

Abbie nodded, excitement lighting through her. Derek grinned, one that promised wickedness and pleasure. "Good girl."

Desire and need thrummed through her veins at his praise, and Abbie obeyed his command. Derek lowered his mouth to her breast and licked her already pebbled nipple before he blew a breath against it. Abbie moaned and gripped the pillow tight.

Derek skimmed his hands along her sides and hips, and pressed kisses down her body. He moved tantalizingly slow. Abbie took in the sight of him worshipping her body. She wanted to commit every second to memory, every searing touch, every sweep of his lips, the exquisite pleasure. Everything.

He teased her folds, edging away from the release Abbie was so desperate for. She ground against his hand, hips up off the bed. Derek tsked. "Patience is a virtue."

"We just spent four days in sin and debauchery. Virtue has long since disappeared."

Derek huffed a laugh.

As soon as Derek's tongue reached her aching core, her climax started to build low in Abbie's belly. Derek was thorough and tender in his ministrations. It didn't take long for Abbie to nearly shred the pillow as her orgasm erupted and she shattered into bliss.

Derek stroked her through the pleasure, his fingers strong and steady. "God, you're beautiful when you come for me."

Abbie shuddered then lay boneless. "That was incredible."

Derek climbed up the bed and captured her mouth. The searing kiss felt like a brand on her heart. "*You're* incredible, Abbie."

CHAPTER 12

Her body deliciously sore, Abbie nestled on Derek's chest. Derek had propped himself up against the headboard, and he stroked her arm. "You know, those clothes aren't going to pack themselves."

He pulled her in tighter. "You're saying you want to get out of bed and pack?"

"I don't want to, but the car is going to be here soon. I need to."

Derek gave one more squeeze, then made to get up. "I'll let you pack. I think I've distracted you enough."

She got up on her knees, the sheets pooled around her, and pulled him down for a quick kiss. "It was the perfect distraction." He dressed quickly and closed the door behind him.

She untangled herself from the sheets, grabbed the sketchbook and pulled free the page with the drawing of him asleep and placed it on his pillow. A little something for him to remember her.

Abbie let out a deep breath and collected her things. It didn't take long, but she still couldn't find that pair of underwear that Derek had taken off in the limo.

Well, if he wanted to keep them, then she'd keep something of his, too. She spotted the blue Henley he'd worn the day before and grabbed it. It still smelled like him, like leather and citrus, and a hint of earthiness.

Abbie took her shirt off and pulled on the Henley. The sleeves were too long, and it fell to just past her ass, but she was determined to wear it home.

A small knock sounded, and Derek opened the door. "Hey, Abbie, the car will – is that my shirt?"

She looked down, then back up at him, eyes wide. "No?"

Derek raised an eyebrow and moved to stand in front of her. He ran his finger along the collar of the shirt, into the small dip caused by the open buttons. "It looks good on you, Abbie."

It was difficult to think. "I'm glad you like it. I was hoping to keep it…if that's okay."

Sadness crossed his features, and Abbie's heart broke at the look. "It's all yours."

Abbie could barely breathe. "What…what were you saying when you came in? About the car?"

Derek dropped his hand. "It'll be here in a few minutes." He looked as though he wanted to say something, but the only thing that came out was, "Are you ready?"

No. "Yes."

"I'll carry your bags out for you." He picked up her two small bags and headed to the front of the house.

Abbie followed him, her heart breaking into small pieces behind her. The car had pulled around to the front, and Derek loaded her bags into the trunk as she stood by the car door.

There was so much she wanted to say, words that built up in her chest but caught in her throat. Could there be more between them than a weekend of amazing sex?

Time. Abbie needed more *time*. Time with him…time to think. Derek had caught her off-guard and she hadn't been prepared to fall for him.

But he would be off to another country for the next few weeks, then who knew after that. The scrutiny of celebrity life aside, there was no way she could compare to the successful actresses and directors and writers he worked with regularly. It would just open the door for even more heartbreak.

Derek came around the car to stand in front of her. She steeled her spine as best she could, shutting down the desperate sadness.

"It's been great, sweets."

"Time to get back to reality, I guess." She tried for humor, but it landed flat between them, splattered on the concrete driveway.

The world stood still as Derek pulled her in by her hips, his lips soft as he pressed them to hers. "Goodbye, Abbie," he whispered.

Tears threatened to fall, and she stepped away before they could. "Goodbye, Derek." She climbed into the back seat, and Derek closed the door behind her. She kept her eyes forward as the driver pulled away from the house, her heart shattered along the driveway behind her.

CHAPTER 13

It was Friday night, and Abbie had invited her best friend Megan for a girls night in: booze, pizza, dessert, and movies. The three days at work had dragged Abbie down under stacks of paperwork and distraction.

But the last few nights had been lonesome and full of tears and ice cream.

Tonight, she needed her best friend, and Abbie had bought a couple extra bottles of wine for the evening. There was a convention tomorrow that Abbie was attending as a vendor, and she still needed to do some prep before bed.

"You really miss him, don't you?" Megan took a sip of her white wine and pushed the bottle closer to Abbie. Abbie's own glass was almost empty. Again.

"No, not really." She poured more wine. Abbie had cleaned off her kitchen table before Megan came over, but really, she'd just moved the stacks of mail and random nonsense to the counter instead.

"Liar."

Abbie sighed. The strained goodbye with Derek had been

brief, but she could have sworn she saw him hesitate before he'd closed her car door. It didn't matter.

"Fine, I miss him. But that was always going to happen."

"True. Spend a weekend with a hot guy and you miss the sex. But do you miss the sex, or do you miss *him?*"

Megan asked the question Abbie had been avoiding for the last few days. Abbie continued to avoid it. Denial might not be a river in Egypt, but Abbie had zero problem navigating it. "Does it matter?"

"Oh, Abbie." Megan shook her head but didn't say anything else.

She did miss him, of course, but her fear of that level of scrutiny was more than enough for her to keep clear of Derek. There were only so many times a person could hear they don't measure up before they decide not to bother trying.

"Have you texted him?" Megan got up to grab the plate of cupcakes she'd brought over and sat back down across from Abbie.

"It's only been a few days. No, I haven't." Abbie took another long drink of her wine and started on one of the cupcakes.

"Has he texted you?" Megan was too smart for her own good.

"Only to say he had a great time and to thank me."

"And you didn't reply?"

"What am I going to say? 'Thanks for the best sex of my life, sorry you're a movie star and I'm not but I'll miss your cock forever?'" It was true, she would miss the sex. Though Abbie would miss the way Derek made her feel confident, safe, sexy, and like what she wanted or didn't want was valid.

He never once made her feel like she wasn't enough.

"It'd be a good place to start!"

Abbie waved her hand in the air. "Oh, don't be ridiculous. I'm not going to text him. I'm not going to be that girl."

"Here we go again with the 'that girl' nonsense."

"It's not nonsense! I don't have to have a meltdown just

because I'm not dating a guy." Abbie finished the first cupcake and started in on a second. Abbie was excellent with cookies, but she was no match for Megan's cupcakes. She swore up and down that Megan put crack in them.

"First off, no woman wants to be the one to have a breakdown after a breakup, so stop it with the 'that girl' bullshit, okay? It's a lie fed to us by movies, and you know it. I'll forgive it this time because you're drunk and heartbroken."

Abbie just huffed in response. "I'm not drunk." She couldn't get too drunk; she still had to prep for the convention tomorrow.

Megan reached across the small table and grabbed Abbie's hand. "But, Abbie, sweetie, it's me. You know you can tell me literally anything. Could there have been something more between you two?"

"Pfft. I don't know. Maybe." Abbie waved her hand and tried to dismiss what Megan said. There was no way she'd admit to anyone there was an excellent possibility that Derek could have been the love of her life, and she'd let him go. "I wouldn't even know what to say to him now."

Megan grabbed Abbie's hand. "You could start with 'Hi, that was a great weekend. I miss you.'"

"He belongs with someone from that world. Someone who can keep up with his lifestyle – the constant moving and the months apart and movie premieres and whatever. That's not me."

Megan snorted. "That's bullshit. You are whoever you want to be, Abs. You wanted to sell your own artwork, and now you're doing it. You wanted to start your own business, and you did." Megan pointed at Abbie and continued, "You put your mind to something, decided what you wanted to do, wanted to be, and did it. That's huge." Megan had never once made their friendship feel like work or like Abbie wasn't good enough.

"It's not like I'm supporting myself with it. I still need to keep my day job." Indeed, her day job as a paralegal in a law firm was boring as hell but it kept a roof over her head and food in her fridge.

"Okay, so what? There are people who live their entire lives working a job they hate, dreaming of doing something creative but are too afraid to try. You did it. So don't tell me that you can't find a way to solve your concerns and be with the man you clearly love."

According to her therapist, Abbie's desire to be better stemmed from growing up in an environment where her family always compared her to others who were always a step ahead. It was obvious after hearing it come from someone else, but she'd never realized it before. There was always competition, usually not very subtle, and it drove Abbie to strive for perfection. If she couldn't achieve it, what was the point?

Until Megan had convinced her to sell her artwork.

But Abbie knew that Derek's life in front of the cameras demanded perfection – social media and tabloids had all but ensured that anyone who dated a celebrity would be under scrutiny and any flaws exposed would be mocked.

That was the last thing Abbie wanted. It was bad enough her own family felt she wasn't good enough, that she didn't measure up. If the world said the same thing, Abbie didn't know how she would bear it.

At least, that was how she felt before she met Derek. Now she wasn't so sure. It had been so easy with him, not just physically. Abbie had never once felt like she didn't measure up in any way with him. If she could get over that issue, maybe she could get over the fear of having her private life in the public eye.

Megan got up to get a cupcake and leaned against the counter. "Abbie, trust me when I say that man is head over heels for you, as he should be."

"How could you know that?"

"Because you told me what he said – that he questioned how he was going to give you up. A guy doesn't say that to someone he isn't emotionally involved with." Megan took a bite of her dessert. "You went after your dream of being an artist and selling your work. You did it – yes, it's small right now but you're doing it. So why not go after your dream guy?"

Maybe Megan had a point. She was usually right. It was infuriating even as Abbie was grateful for her friend's insight.

Abbie smiled. "I'll think about it." She blew out a breath. "In the meantime, I need to prep for tomorrow's show. I got in some boxes I need to sort through and organize. *And* I have to make sure everything is packed."

"I wish I could keep you company, but Tucker is coming into town tomorrow and asked if one of his friends could crash on my couch. I'll be cleaning tonight and playing hostess all weekend."

"Tell Tucker I said hi." Abbie hadn't seen either of Megan's older brothers, Tucker and Liam, in a while. Liam had moved to Virginia to pursue a job after college and Tucker was a teacher somewhere in NYC. "Do you know what friend he has coming over?" Abbie threw out her cupcake wrappers and followed Megan out of the kitchen.

"No clue. But it's Tucker, so it's likely a girl he's dating that he's too scared to bring home." Megan grabbed her bag from the couch and headed to the door.

"Good luck with that."

"Call me after the convention and we'll catch up."

"Will do. Bye, hun." Abbie gave Megan a squeeze and closed and locked the door behind her.

She eyed the stack of boxes next to the door and sighed. Thoughts of Derek and their weekend together swirled in her head.

Abbie had felt more empowered and confident in herself that weekend than she had with anyone else she'd ever dated. She'd accredited it to the fact that it was one weekend, and they'd never see each other again.

She almost took her phone out to text him, but she hesitated.

Abbie had to focus on the convention tomorrow, hopefully make some sales. Then she would reach out to him.

She set about organizing her things for the next day and two hours later, everything was packed, organized, and in the back of her car. Ready to collapse, Abbie undressed, set her alarm, and climbed into bed.

Exhaustion was heavy, but thoughts of Derek and their weekend together kept her from sleep. He'd never outright said that he wanted a relationship with her. That should be enough of a hint, right? It shouldn't matter that she couldn't stop thinking about him and kept having dreams of him and their weekend, should it?

There were plenty of celebrities who were able to keep their relationships private. The only thing Abbie needed to do was decide. If there was a way to address her privacy concerns, to keep her life as far from the spotlight as possible, would she want to be with him?

The answer was staggeringly easy.

Yes.

Megan's words from earlier rang in Abbie's mind. "You went after your dream of being an artist and selling your work. Why not go after your dream guy?"

Megan was right. Fear shouldn't stop Abbie from going after what she wanted. Love was worth the risk.

The Long Island Art, Comic, and Fantasy Convention was one of Abbie's favorites. She'd attended as a fan for years before opening her own little shop and selling her artwork.

This was her second year as a vendor, and so she knew a few of the other artists and vendors. A lot of them were often at other local town fairs together, and Abbie loved the little community they were building amongst themselves.

The convention was crowded, and Abbie had a buzz all day from the energy. One of her favorite parts was meeting new people, even if she didn't make a sale.

Abbie's artwork mostly consisted of quotes from popular books in the fantasy and romance genres with designs that matched the aesthetic of the books. The readership for both genres were voracious and her small social media accounts for the artwork had been steadily growing. It was the only public account she had, and it was because Megan had forced her into it.

By the end of the day, she had fewer prints and pins to bring home and a bunch of new followers on social media. It was more than she'd hoped for.

Just as Abbie started to pack up, when the last of the customers were winding their way out of the room specially designated for the artists, Megan appeared at the table.

"Megs! What are you doing here?" She hugged her friend across the table. "What happened to your house guest?"

"He's off somewhere with Tucker. I didn't ask questions."

Abbie's jaw almost hit the floor, especially as Megan's cheeks turned red. "He?"

Megan waved a hand in the air. "Details later. I figured I'd come help you pack up and maybe we can grab food."

Abbie was worn out, but Megan was always a bright spot. "That'd be great. And you can tell me all about this 'he' that's staying on your couch."

"There's not much to tell." Megan came around and started to take pins off the board and lay them out on the table. "His name is Caleb. He's tall and quiet."

Abbie noticed Megan moving a little slowly. "You can just put those in the containers under the table. I'll organize them later." Megan nodded and reached for the clear containers Abbie used.

The rest of the vendors packed up and a few stopped by to chat as she and Megan worked together to clear up the space. Megan had gotten into a particularly animated conversation with one of the other artists when Abbie was finally done getting everything onto her little handcart.

The sun was going to set soon, and she wanted to be on the road by the time it got dark. "Meg, I don't mean to interrupt, but I'm going to go put this stuff in my car."

She started to walk away but Megan said, "Have you met Abbie? She's the artist at this table."

Abbie tried not to groan too loudly as she gingerly set the handcart upright and turned to say hi.

"Abbie, this is Rachel. Rachel, Abbie." Megan motioned from one to the other.

Abbie smiled as she shook Rachel's extended hand. "It's nice to meet you, Rachel."

Rachel's smile was wide. "You, too! I'm actually a fan of your work!" Her red hair was pulled back into a bun, much like Abbie's own hair.

Abbie blushed. "Thank you. I'm sorry but I don't know if I'm familiar with your work."

Rachel stepped back, her smile still big. "That's okay! I'm a new artist, so probably not. This is my first ever show."

Abbie was ready to get home and into some comfortable pants, but didn't want to be rude, especially not to a new artist. Abbie herself still felt like a complete newbie. "That's amazing. Do you have a card? I'd love to check out your stuff."

"Really? Yes, I do. Hang on a second." Rachel ran back to her table, about thirty feet down the aisle.

"She's talented." Megan said. "I saw some of her stuff as I was coming down before and really liked it. It's nice that you asked for her card."

If only Megan knew that it was Abbie's way to get out of the conversation as quickly as possible and home to her cozy pants. And down a glass or two of wine as she figured out how to text Derek.

"She's nice. I always like to meet new artists."

Rachel came back with her card, and Abbie thanked her as she put it in her pocket. "It was great to meet you, Rachel. Hopefully we'll see you again at another Con."

"You, too!" Rachel turned and said her goodbyes to Megan. Abbie went back to her handcart and hoisted it onto the wheels.

"Why are you in such a rush, Abs?" Megan grabbed their purses and walked along as Abbie pushed the cart to the exit. A moment later there was a crash and a curse behind her.

She turned to see Megan sprawled on the floor, half the contents of their bags surrounding her, and an overturned small trashcan. Abbie couldn't help but laugh as she went to help Megan up.

"You know it's the sneaky trash cans you have to watch out for, Megs."

Megan scoffed and grabbed the contents of her purse and shoved them inside.

They were almost to the door, things in hand, when Abbie whispered, "I'm in a rush because I decided to text Derek."

Megan squealed, and practically bounced in place.

"Oh my god, shhh." Abbie's cheeks warmed when she saw a few people glance their way. "This is why I wasn't going to say anything until we were alone."

"So, basically what you're saying is that you know I'm right."

"I wouldn't go *that* far." But Abbie laughed anyway.

They were out the door, the sun slipping behind the trees, and Abbie led the way to her car. She'd parked in the small vendor lot around the side of the building.

Abbie turned the corner and the world stopped spinning.

Derek leaned against her car.

Abbie stopped so short that a couple of containers fell off her cart. She barely registered Megan retrieving them and putting them back.

Derek's legs were crossed at the ankles, hands tucked into his jean pockets, his face obscured by a blue baseball cap and sunglasses.

Abbie would know him anywhere.

"Breathe." Megan whispered. Abbie took a breath in, unaware that her lungs had stopped working. There was a duffel bag on the ground next to him.

Abbie looked at her friend. "Did you...?"

Megan's smile answered the question. "I'll let the muscle help you load these. Byeee." She waved to Derek and disappeared back around the building to the lot for the public.

Abbie still hadn't moved. Derek pushed off the back of her car and crossed the short distance.

There was a soft smile on his face, and those blue eyes danced. "Hi, beautiful."

CHAPTER 14

Abbie didn't know what to say first. So, she went with the obvious. "What are you doing here? How…how did you know I'd be here?"

"You posted that you'd be here for the show. I flew in last night." He reached for the handle of her cart and took it from her.

"You flew into town last night…for the convention? I didn't know you were a guest."

"I wasn't."

"Then why would you…" Abbie stopped as a thought occurred to her. She hadn't given it enough consideration; she'd been too afraid.

Derek put the cart to the side, stood in front of her, and tipped her chin up to look at him. "I missed you."

Abbie's heart melted. "I missed you, too."

Derek's gaze left hers for a moment to look behind her. He took a step back, ducked his head ever so slightly, and said, "Can I help you to your car? And maybe ask for a ride?"

Off balance for a moment at the sudden loss of Derek's warmth, Abbie heard people laughing behind her. Derek slipped his arm through hers as Abbie turned to see the last few of the vendors come around the building. Abbie waved at them before heading in the direction of her car with Derek.

Everything loaded into the trunk and backseat, Abbie sat in the driver seat and let the car idle. She kept her hands in her lap, gripped together so she didn't reach over and take off his hat so she could run her fingers through his hair.

"I can't believe you're here." She waved at the building behind them. "That you came to the show and waited outside. Oh shit, how long did you wait?" It wasn't too hot yet but if he'd been there for a long time...

"I didn't want to risk anyone noticing me inside. I didn't wait long, I promise."

"No, it's not that. It's just...I can't believe you're here." Abbie didn't think twice. She wasn't about to walk away or let him leave without at least a conversation about a future together. "Do you want to come over for dinner?"

"I'd love to."

It would be easier to discuss things over food, anyway. Thirty minutes later they were on the floor of her living room, takeout boxes arranged carefully between them on the small brown ottoman she'd carried from place to place since college.

She cringed as Derek moved a box full of clear plastic sleeves away from his back. "I'm sorry this place is such a mess. I was in a rush last night packing for the show and it was late, and I fell asleep before I could clean up."

Derek shuffled his container around a little bit. "You don't need to apologize. You should see what my place looks like when I pack before going on location. You're allowed to live in your space without excuse, Abbie."

Words failed her, so she smiled softly and looked away. Being near him again had her all in a tizzy, and it was all she could do not to touch him.

"Before we eat, uh, I brought something for you from

London." Derek stood and went over to the duffel bag he had dropped by the front door.

"You brought me something from London?" She didn't have any sort of gift for him. Was she supposed to? "You didn't have to do that."

As Derek sat next to her, he handed her a flat package wrapped in plain brown paper. There was a red bow attached to the top left corner with her name written in a messy hand underneath.

"I saw it and thought of you." He brushed his knuckles along her cheek, his voice barely a whisper. "I haven't been able to stop thinking about you. It's been incredibly distracting."

It was hard to breathe. Abbie tilted her head up ever so slightly, lips parted, a silent invitation.

Derek flicked his gaze to her mouth, then up to meet her eyes. Desire shone in those blue depths. He licked his lips, teeth dragging along the bottom one. He placed a single kiss on her cheek. "Open your present. Then I'll open mine." He trailed his fingers down her arm, igniting every nerve ending in her body.

Abbie suppressed a shiver of anticipation and focused on the wrapped gift in her lap. She pulled apart the tape at the edges and opened the brown paper to reveal a suede-covered book tied closed with a string. Abbie opened it and flipped through the pages. Blank.

A sketchbook.

She gasped, tears in her eyes. "It's beautiful. Thank you."

"I'm glad you like it." He blew out a breath. "I know how talented you are, and it's important for talented people to have the tools they need."

"It's the most thoughtful gift anyone has gotten me." Abbie reached to place a small kiss on his cheek. "I love it," she whispered.

She lingered, just for a moment. Abbie went to move away but Derek slid his arm around her waist and held her close. His head dipped to the sensitive spot behind her ear, his lips against her skin.

"I loved my sketch, by the way. Thank you for leaving it for me." His voice was barely above a whisper.

Abbie swallowed hard. "You're welcome."

"Can I unwrap you now?" Huskiness lined his voice. His fingers tracing along her spine provided sufficient distraction, but Abbie shook her head. Derek stopped moving. Abbie wasn't sure he even breathed.

"I need to say something first."

She didn't know how to say it. She'd never told anyone she was in a relationship with that she loved them. She'd cared about them, absolutely, but she'd never fallen as completely in love with them as she had with Derek.

"Um, I, uh...I don't know how to say this. So, I'm going to just..." She looked at him, at his ocean-blue eyes, and remembered that she'd never felt like she was drowning. No, she'd always felt safe, swept away by passion or desire, but anchored all the same. By him.

She dove in and went right past her fear. "I love you. I'm *in* love with you. I want to make it work with us, even with all the things that scare me. They don't scare me as much anymore, not if it means I get to be with you." It all came out in a rush, and Abbie was breathless when she'd finished.

Derek's eyes were alight with joy. "I love you too, Abbie."

Abbie felt lighter than she had in years. "You do?" She couldn't quite believe it, even as the words settled into her heart.

He nodded. "Yes, I do. Exactly as you are." Derek held his hand out, an invitation. She accepted, and he clasped his other hand on top. "I know there are things about my life that worry you, and I promise to do everything I can to make sure you feel safe and your life is as private as you want."

Her throat closed and tears started to flow. Derek brushed them away with his thumb.

"I appreciate that more than I can say. I'm less afraid now. You've always made me feel safe." Abbie took a shuddering breath in. "I do have a couple of questions."

"Anything."

"How are we going to handle the issue of our privacy?"

Derek's hands settled on her waist, his gaze earnest. "My manager and agent will have some suggestions. What's your biggest concern? The thing you're most scared of?"

"I don't want every detail of my life online, for the world to see and judge. I'm scared of the scrutiny, and not going to lie...a little bit for my – our – safety. We're not royalty or anything, I know, but security isn't something to sniff at."

"It definitely isn't. We can figure out the security part a little later – that's something my manager can help with." He gently stroked her cheek, and she leaned into his touch. "As for keeping your life away from the public eye, nothing needs to change about the way you live your life, Abbie. Not if you don't want it to."

"But what about going out on dates? To restaurants or movies?"

"We'll have to ask some people who know how to maneuver, but I think we'll be okay. Plus, I'm more of a stay in and eat kind of guy, you know."

Abbie blushed. She did know.

"Red carpet events?"

"You don't have to walk the carpet with me if you don't want to. I'd love for you to come to premieres, but there's a separate entrance that you can go into. And it's rare for photos from those to get leaked. Security is pretty high at events like that."

She thought for a few moments. It'd be fun to wear a pretty dress and get all dolled up for a night, even if she didn't walk the carpet for photos. Then again, it might be nice to declare to the world that she was with Derek.

"Would you want me to walk the red carpet with you?"

"Only if you want to. It's intense. I'll never ever force you to go in front of cameras, Abbie."

A weight lifted off her chest. "I don't know if I can handle the intensity of that."

"You make that decision, not me."

Derek adjusted his body on the floor, sat up a little straighter, and moved her so that she was straddling his waist. Abbie ran her fingers through his hair and took in every detail of his face: his strong jaw, perfect cheekbones, and the bluest eyes she'd ever seen. She still had difficulty believing he was in front of her.

Derek continued to trace his fingers up and down her back, every now and again daring to graze the side of her breasts. "You know, I really missed you, Abbie."

"Oh?"

"Mhm." He leaned forward to place a kiss on her neck. "You've been all I could think about." His lips left a trail of fire down the column of her neck.

"I thought about you every night." He was here, real and in front of her. Desire spread through her as she gave him access to more of her. "I would touch myself, and imagine it was your hands or your lips on me. And it was your name on my lips when I came."

"Fuck, Abbie." Derek threaded a hand through her hair, and the other gripped around her back.

Derek kissed her, a deep kiss that promised passion and heat. Abbie needed him, needed his skin against hers, his body moving with hers.

She broke apart their kiss, Derek leaning forward for more. "My bedroom is right down the hall, with a very large and comfortable bed."

"Are you sure?"

"Absolutely." She kissed him again, nibbled his bottom lip, and rolled her hips against the bulge in his pants. He groaned, and a spark of desire ran through her veins.

"Then after you, sweets."

Abbie stood up and led him down the hall. She lifted the hem of her shirt and pulled it over her head as she walked backward. The look of shock on Derek's face when he saw the black lace bra she'd chosen this morning sent a thrill of electricity through her.

"Please tell me there's a matching pair of underwear."

"What do you think?" She winked at him and held out her hand. He followed, caging her against the wall at her back.

"I think you like to play dirty."

"You might just be right about that." Abbie pulled his shirt up and ran her nails along his chest and abs. She reached up and nibbled his ear again, then ducked under his arm and backed up to the door of her bedroom.

Derek groaned and gave chase. "You're trying to kill me, aren't you?"

A giggle escaped her, and she turned the handle to her room and stepped in. She held her hand in invitation and Derek followed. Abbie backed up in the small space until her legs hit the bed, Derek keeping pace.

Derek lifted her chin and leaned in to capture her mouth. Abbie moaned and threaded her fingers through his hair. She delighted in the silky softness.

"Abbie?"

"Hmm?"

His voice was a rough whisper as he asked, "Can I unwrap you now? I want to taste you."

Abbie was already wet and throbbing for him, her skin hot and flushed. "Yes. Please, yes." She started to undo her belt, but Derek's fingers were there.

"Let me." A simple command, but Abbie had to force her knees not to buckle. She nodded and moved her hands to her sides.

Derek's movements were deft and swift, and a moment later

he tugged her jeans off each leg. He sucked in a breath at the sight of the black panties trimmed with pink lace.

Derek went to his knees in front of her and placed a reverent kiss on the inside of each thigh. Abbie sucked in a breath with each. When Derek licked her for the first time, Abbie dropped against the bed and moaned his name.

"You taste even better than I remember."

"Fuck, Derek."

"Not yet. I want to eat my fill first." He licked and sucked on her clit, and all thoughts evaporated from Abbie's head. She was nothing but the feeling of him worshipping her, and electricity flowed through her veins.

Her orgasm swelled and swelled. Derek slipped a finger inside and stroked that perfect spot. Once, twice, and the third time sent her over the edge.

Abbie's hips bucked off the bed as pleasure tore through her, but Derek's hand kept her still. He was merciless in wringing out every morsel of her climax with his tongue and expert fingers.

When she finally settled back into herself and could breathe again, she laughed. "Wow."

Derek looked up from where he still knelt. "I've missed that." He crawled up the bed until he was over her body and gave her a deep kiss. "I've missed *you*, Abbie."

"I missed you, too." She placed her lips against his and pulled him down on top of her. "I need you, Derek." Abbie whispered it in his ear; her hand reached between their bodies and wrapped around his thick cock.

"Christ, Abbie."

"Fuck me all night, Derek. Please, I need you to fuck me."

He kissed her again, and Abbie was lost to the feel of him. "Whatever you wish, Abbie."

EPILOGUE

Three months later

"If we're going to do this, we need to do it right." Derek's face was all serious concentration as he looked at his phone. They'd spent more time apart than together over the last few months, and Abbie had missed him while he was working. Video calls, phone calls, and text messages just weren't as satisfying as touching him. Still, exploring their relationship and their feelings had outweighed the cost – including the public aspect of his life.

"You know, if we weren't talking about food, that could be taken in a very, very sexual way."

"Then it's a shame we're talking about food."

Abbie nudged him but laughed anyway. "We could go to my cousin's diner. It's not too far, and the breakfast food there is off the charts."

"I thought we were looking for a late-night snack. It's almost eleven."

"Diners serve breakfast all day. Most of them do, anyway. It's a thing. Plus, my cousin's place is open until two in the morning."

Derek put his arm around her shoulder. "Are you sure you want our first public appearance together as a couple to be at your cousin's diner?"

She loved his consideration. "Yes, I'm sure. One of the ways I can handle my fear is if I control how and when I'm seen with you. The rest is noise, right?"

"Right." He kissed her on the forehead.

"I want to take you there. And it could also be good for business, right?" She held her hands up like she was showcasing a headline, "'Famous actor Derek Hartley loves the French toast at The Starfire Diner.' They'll be so busy they won't know what to do with themselves."

"You wanna give them a heads-up we're coming?"

She nodded. "Good idea." Abbie sent off a long text to her cousin and added a request to sit in one of the back booths and for some of the tables nearby to be moved away.

Abbie motioned to his phone. "Look up the menu, but they'll make anything you want."

"Honestly, you made the French toast sound delicious just now."

"You won't regret it. Add some bacon on the side, or the corned beef hash. Mm, incredible."

"Most people might think you're crazy, you know, the way you talk about breakfast food." Derek booped her nose.

"Good thing you're not most people."

"No, I am not. Let's go eat."

The diner had been in her family for years, and it felt like home. The ten-minute ride through her hometown of Starfire Lake flew by. Derek insisted he drive, but she won out with the argument that she knew the area and it would just be easier.

Her cousin, Dimitri, met them at the register, just inside the front door. "Welcome to the Starfire Diner." Dimitri held out a hand, a huge smile on his face. "We're honored to have you, Mr. Hartley."

Derek shook Dimitri's hand, matching her cousin's smile. "Derek, please."

"Derek, then. Right this way. We have a booth ready for you."

Dimitri led the way, and Abbie followed the two of them around to the back of the diner. Derek waited for her to slide into the booth before sitting across from her. The door to the kitchen was just a few feet behind Derek, and Abbie could see the busboys and line cooks jockeying to see out the little round window. They were lucky they didn't topple through the swinging door.

"Here are your menus, and Niko will be right over with some water and to get your drink order. Please, if there's anything you need, just let me know."

"We will, Dimi." Abbie smiled up at her cousin, glad she'd told him they were coming. "Thanks, for everything." She nodded at the rest of the room.

He'd cleared out the tables in the dining room, leaving only the booths against the opposite wall and the booth behind her. She made a mental note to leave a huge tip for Niko, if he was losing that many potential tables.

"Anything for you, yeah?"

"Tell the guys in the back they can come say hi if they want, before they break their necks at the door." Abbie laughed.

Derek turned around to look where she'd indicated. They all disappeared.

"If they want autographs or pics, I'd be happy to do that for them."

She smiled at Derek, but Dimi looked aghast. "Oh, we won't bother you like that."

"He means it, Dimi. It's fine."

"Ah, here comes Niko. Call me if you need anything. I'll be up front."

They ordered French toast with extra bacon on the side, some home fries, and drinks. The busboys did get their photos, and

Abbie laughed at the shock on their faces when Derek suggested they tag him in their posts.

As soon as Niko brought their food, Derek dug in to the French toast, barely adding butter or syrup.

"You were right, Abbie. This is the best French toast I've had in I don't know how long. I wonder why it's so good."

She took a bite of her own and smiled. "It's a family secret, apparently. Not even I know!"

While they were eating, the booths on the opposite end of the diner filled up. Both groups looked to be in their twenties, and they all nudged each other when they caught sight of Derek. Nerves were a small hiccup in Abbie's stomach, but she pushed them aside. Derek and his manager had done absolutely everything to make her feel comfortable.

Tonight was about them being together. And breakfast food. She focused on Derek and laughed as he inhaled his food, nerves and worries fading to the furthest corner of her mind.

Derek glanced up at Abbie, concern shading his eyes. "You okay?"

Her fear didn't loom as large when Derek was with her.

Grateful she'd chosen love over fear, Abbie reached over and grabbed his hand. She brought it to her mouth and brushed his knuckles with a kiss. "I'm happier than I've ever been."

ACKNOWLEDGMENTS

Husband – without your support and encouragement, I would have given up on writing a long time ago. Thank you for reminding me that I can do the thing. I love you more than words can say. Purple popsicles forever, my love.

Chipmunk – you are the light of my life. I hope you know that you can do hard things, and that mama will always be there when you need. I love you.

My wifey – you are the best friend a girl could have. I love you so much, on fish fingers and custard.

My writing community – Jeannie Moon, Patty Blount, Stacey Agdern, Violet Vahle, and everyone in the Long Island Romance Writers, thank you for the endless support, advice, encouragement, and love. I wouldn't be where I am today without you.

Michele Lang – I don't know what I would do without you. I adore you and am lucky to call you my friend.

Melissa Wolfe – the Ann Perkins to my Leslie Knope, I am so glad that you're in my life. Thank you for telling me like it is. Stay golden.

Blue Saffire – you are the best. Thank you for your time and generosity. I couldn't have done this without you kicking my butt.

Zoe York – thank you for listening to my insanity and providing insight on so many things! And for welcoming me into the supportive & warm community you created.

Carrie Lomax – I can't thank you enough for reading an early version of this book and giving your honest feedback. This book would not be what it is without you.

Holland Rae – I wouldn't have gotten through revisions with any semblance of sanity without you. Thank you for late night Zooms. You are such a source of light and inspiration and support.

Rebecca – Your beta read and copy editing was invaluable. This book would not exist in its final form without your insight. Thank you.

Stephanie B. – Thank you so much for being such a cheerleader and supportive friend.

Kristina P. – Your proofreading was fantastic, and I am so grateful. Thank you, friend. Any typos are entirely mine.

Naomi Lane – your talent is exceptional, and I am so glad we get to work together. My book cover is beautiful, and I cannot thank you enough.

My family and friends – thank you for lifting me up and supporting me. I love you all.

And my two constant companions, Nyx and Lila – you make every day a constant surprise. Thank you for keeping me company into the wee hours as I worked. Mama loves you.

I am so very lucky to do this. My high school self would be jumping up and down in the kitchen. I couldn't have done it without her dream.

There are so many people without whom this book would not exist, and if I left someone off the list, please know it was not intentional – I am just really, really bad at remembering things, and I hope you'll forgive me.

ABOUT THE AUTHOR

Though she grew up on Long Island, Vivi Parish now lives in the suburbs of Texas with her husband, toddler, and two very sweet dogs. You can find Vivi active on social media posting photos of her dogs and daily life.

Be sure to sign up for her newsletter for book updates. You can find her on social media here.

Her website is www.viviparish.com.